WEAPON FROM THE STARS

By
ROG PHILLIPS

I0616685

ARMCHAIR FICTION
PO Box 4369, Medford, Oregon 97504

*For more information about Armchair Books and products, visit our
website at...*

www.armchairfiction.com

Or email us at...

armchairfiction@yahoo.com

GALACTIC INTRIGUE AT ITS BEST...

It didn't take Henry Prince long to realize he was in over his head. His assignment had seemed simple: find some subversives and report them to headquarters. Finding them had been easy. And finding a couple of loyal buddies to help watch his back had seemed a blessing. But then things started getting...strange. Magic summoning coins; shadowy characters that could appear and disappear at will; enigmatic meetings with questionable intent...what was going on here that Henry Prince was somehow missing?

Sci-fi great Rog Phillips spins a great intergalactic tale filled with mystery that will perhaps leave you baffled and confused, because what do we truly know in regards to Heaven and Hell?

FOR A SECOND COMPLETE NOVEL, TURN TO PAGE 85

CAST OF CHARACTERS

HENRY "HANK" PRINCE

He was a good undercover agent looking for subversives. What he found was a whole lot more than he'd expected.

JOSEPH WRIGHT

He'd signed up for this job to earn some dough. But when intrigue and romance knocked at his door—he met it head on.

AL

Here was a man who paid attention to detail, a much-needed asset when dealing with conspiracy and murder.

HONEY CHILDS

Oh…but her kisses were sweet. A blonde bombshell of heavenly beauty, could it be she had the devil inside?

PAUL AND HARRY

Troublemakers of the 'saboteur-murder-not-very-bright type," these two needed to be watched…and approached with caution.

ANNAS

A shrewd Lotissivian invader, he had the ability to make one believe in his every word.

MAJOR WINTHROP

Who's side was he on anyway? For a man who promised to protect his agents, he seemed awfully chummy with the enemy.

CHAPTER ONE

"HEY JOE, look at the mail order clerk!" The coarsely built man who had spoken nudged his companion, who turned his eyes, stared in mock astonishment, then burst into loud guffaws.

Henry Prince flushed under their stare, turning away in pretended indifference.

"Look at them pretty fingers," the second man said in overdone admiration. "What's your name, mister?"

"Henry Prince," Henry said politely.

"Henry? Gawd!" Joe turned to his pal. "Think of that, Al. We can't call him Hank because he isn't the type. And *Henry!* Nobody would be caught using the word."

"Leave him alone," someone farther down the line growled. "He's here for the same reason you are; to make enough dough in two years to retire on."

"If we live that long, and come out of it able to enjoy living," another said.

"Cut that out!" another said sharply. "You know damn well there's no radioactivity left there. They wouldn't dare lie about that."

"Oh, wouldn't they?" came the retort. "They'd lie if they couldn't get the workers without lying. Think they could get us, or anybody, if they came right out and said in two years we'd be so radioactive we'd die before we could enjoy what we come away with?"

"Then what are you in this line for?" Al said.

"He's wrong," Henry Prince spoke up. "I've read the details. There was radioactivity, yes. But they've covered the whole ten thousand square miles with fifteen feet of concrete.

That's a perfect shield. They had to or there wasn't any use in starting construction. Nobody could have lived in the building when they finished it."

"Then what do they pay such big wages for?" the stubborn one said, a trifle too loudly. "Why do they keep hiring more men? When will they get enough? What happens to those that've been over there two years already?"

"Yeah," a new voice picked it up. "What's a thousand dollars a day for two years if we don't live to enjoy it?"

"Are you, by any chance," Henry Prince asked, turning to the man, "paid to enter this line and start rumors that will make the men back out?"

"Listen, you little squirt," the stubborn man sneered, "shut up before I knock your teeth loose."

"I see you avoided answering my question," Henry said, a nervous smile flicking across his face.

"Yeah," Joe said, looking at Al and nodding. "Why didn't you answer his question? Picking a fight with the half-pint ain't an answer."

"Ah, shut up," the man said. "I noticed you were trying to pick a fight with him yourself."

"Gentlemen," Henry said. "If he's a hired agent to drive applicants away he'll drop out of line before he reaches the employment office. That way we'll know for sure, and can have him arrested and put in the treason trials."

"The heck you can," the man said, edging out of line. "Me, I'm having no part in putting up this building in what's left of Europe. The rest of you can go over and get poisoned by radioactivity and be damned."

He edged further from the line. The other man who had sided with him was also inching away.

"Get back in line," Al sneered. "You can't back out now."

For answer the two men took to their heels. Instantly Henry Prince was running after them. Al and Joe passed him, each tackling one of the fleeing pair.

When Henry reached them they were rolling and scuffling, the two more intent on escaping than in fighting. Henry chose one pair of fighting men and poised over them. Suddenly he seized a wrist and ducked under it, turning his body as he did so. A man miraculously lifted out of the twisting mass, turning lazily over in the air, to land on his back with a loud thump. What was left of that maelstrom of flesh, namely, Joe, rose with a bewildered expression on his face, watching with something close to awe as Henry repeated his performance on the other pair.

"Now let's all get back in line," Henry said, "before we lose our place."

"Say," Joe said to Henry, "you're all right—Hank!"

"NAME?" the tired man at the desk, asked.

"Henry Prince. The two that came in ahead of me are suspected agents. What're their names?"

"Paul Granch and Harry Lark. They're signed up and can't get away."

"Good," Henry said. "You know my orders. I'll really sign up now and go across with the group."

"Dependents?" the tired man asked, ballpoint pen poised over the blank form on the desk.

"Mother. Marie Prince, 1408 U Street, Novark, Washington."

"Age?"

"Twenty-eight. The two coming in next—Joe and Al—I want with me. On the same plane. In fact, assign them to the same job with me and those two, Paul and Harry."

The questions went on until the sheet was filled out.

"Through that door," the tired man said, pointing with his pen.

Henry went through the door and found himself in a large waiting room whose windows opened onto a concrete strip on which a huge transport plane idled.

The two men named Paul Granch and Harry Lark were together near one of the windows, talking uneasily, their eyes studying the plane and the chained off lane leading to it from the waiting room, with armed guards standing back far enough to bring down anyone who tried to escape.

Henry smiled quietly, merging with the crowd so that he wouldn't be observed. Shortly he sensed someone stop beside him, and looked up. It was Joe, his eyes and coarse face friendly and curious.

"How'd you do it, Hank?" he asked.

Henry blinked his eyes, then comprehension came.

"Oh," he said, "I had a friend who was a jujitsu teacher. It really wasn't anything. I will admit it's the first time I ever tried it on a stranger, though. Unfair, really, but a minute more and we'd all have been arrested."

"You sure you just hired up for general labor?" Joe asked quietly.

"Of course," Henry said, looking surprised. "That's where the money is. The bosses don't make a thousand a day."

"Screwy setup," Joe said conversationally. "Workers get a thousand a day while wages at home are fifteen and twenty a day. And still they can't get workers. Maybe if they only offered thirty a day they'd get more. That doesn't sound like a suicide job then."

"You know the alternative," Henry said. "They're trying to keep from having to conscript labor, and if the Government can't keep on schedule with this construction work by hiring men, and won't conscript labor, then the

Lotissivians will drop an occupation force and make us do it their way."

"Yeah," Joe said glumly. "And what's a thousand a day? They take back nine-tenths of it in income taxes, and the rest is just paper money, easy to print, worthless except that people in business have to accept it."

Al came through the door from the employment office, his eyes surveying the room until they found Joe and Henry. He pushed through the crowd and joined them.

"I think I was the last one on this load," he said. "And what a load! Must be a hundred and fifty in here. If they all go in that plane out there they'd better make the trip quick. There won't be room for a slice of bread to make us sardines into a sandwich." He looked down, at Henry's five-foot-eight from his height of six-five and smiled. "Think you could flip me like you did those two? Never mind, don't show me." He backed off in mock alarm.

"We three'd better stick together," Joe said. "No telling what's ahead, and three's company."

"You mean three's a crowd," Henry said, the corners of his mouth twitching.

"So what, professor?" Joe said. "We may need to be a crowd. Them two we mussed up are just the type to knife us if they get a chance."

"Ever see either of them before?" Henry asked.

"Not me," Joe said.

"Me neither," Al said.

A loud voice broke in from the door to the airport.

"All right," it shouted. "Get moving. I want this room cleared in five minutes. Single file you!"

"Stick together," Joe said softly. "I've got a funny feeling about them two jerks…"

"ALL RIGHT, get moving," a voice somewhere ordered. "This coffin is taking off in ten minutes. Tell the stewardess what you want in the way of eats and drinks on the way in, and be sure you sit in the seat that has your reservation number. Come on, get moving."

Men were moving up the cleated metal ramp, pausing at the open hatchway, then ducking inside. Al led the way, followed by Henry, then Joe. Those behind pushed in gently. Two-thirds of the way up the incline each man turned to take a last look at the New York skyline. It was farewell.

Henry Prince was no exception. Then he was ducking into the plane, looking for the stewardess.

"Move as far forward as you can get," a metallic voice was repeating. There was no stewardess.

Henry jerked his head up to take in the plane's interior. There were no seats. Instead, there were literally hundreds of straps hanging from the arched ceiling of the plane.

"Snap out of it!" the metallic voice barked.

Henry jerked back to the source of the voice. The tail space of the plane was walled off by a metal wall, in which was set a thick transparent window with three round holes whose only purpose could be to insert the barrels of guns for aiming on the occupants of the plane. Behind this window was the owner of the voice erupting from the small loudspeaker attached to the ceiling above the wall.

"It's going to be a terrible hardship," the metallic voice said. "You'll all have to stand for three hours. All the way across the Atlantic. You won't be able to move around. It'll be almost as terrible as the subway, but not quite so jerky. Get moving, you!"

"Come on, Hank," Joe whispered, shoving gently.

They pressed into the wall of bodies, groping upward for a strap to cling to, other bodies pressing them still more solidly into the mass of flesh.

There was the clang of the hatch closing. A whirring noise started up, bringing a steady wind of cool air.

"The jerk back there behind the window's putting on black light glasses," Al whispered. The next instant the lights went out.

There were no port windows. Henry knew that there must be black light bathing them so that the guard could see them clearly while they could see nothing. So much the better.

"Take my hand, Hank," Joe's whisper sounded. "We'll move up a ways so's anybody who's got a line on us can't find us. Easy now."

Henry followed in the wake of the larger man as they inched so slowly they were barely moving. The plane started to move, bouncing over the concrete, its movement aiding their progress.

"This's good enough," Al grunted nearby.

Henry tried to disengage his hand from Joe's. Joe held on.

"Keep hold," he whispered.

They were in the air now, the soft roar of the twelve jet motors deepening. The mass of flesh they were apart of moved under the action of a slow banking turn.

It wasn't bad, Henry decided.

The refreshing draft was growing colder. It was a welcome coldness as the heat from the massed bodies around him began to accumulate.

No one was talking. There was no sound except the jets. Henry's thoughts turned toward the organized mass movement of which he was now an insignificant part. These planes were leaving every two hours, each with a hundred and fifty men. Eighteen hundred men every twenty-four hours, day after day.

That fantastic super-building being constructed was using them all as fast as they could be brought over.

Of what use would such a building be, even to the Lotissivians? A hundred miles square, a hundred miles high. Fifty million square miles of floor space. Equivalent to one-fourth the surface area of the entire world. And set in the heart of devastated Europe near where Vienna once had been.

A tearing scream shattered his thoughts. It was only a few feet away. It was followed by another, then a third, which died shudderingly into a dead silence in which even the roar of the jets seemed to retreat.

The jet roar came back, pounding into the silence, dispersing it. But in the total darkness there was no movement, no sound. Nothing but the press of unmoving bodies, the firm grip of Joe's fingers about Henry's hand.

"It's a knife in him," a voice whispered in horror. Then the voice changed to a panic stricken blubbering. "He's bleeding on me! Get him away! Oh God, get him away!"

There was the thud of a fist...

HENRY PRINCE began to experience the full horror of utter darkness. Or rather, he began to sense it. And from the way Joe's grip on his hand was increasing he knew that he wasn't the only one to feel it. His imagination tortured him with visions of a murderer sliding between bodies, searching for him.

Him? The screams of the dying man had come from about where he had been standing when the lights went out. Had that knife been meant for him? Joe and Al had been smart, moving to a different place after the lights went out.

Who were Joe and Al? Just a couple of laborers? Would men who had just worked at jobs requiring muscles all their lives think of the possibility of murder in the dark?

His thoughts went back to when Al and Joe had been poking fun at him. That had been a bullying sort of thing, not in keeping with their actions and attitude since then. But a harmless sort of bullying. As understandable in two coarse giants as their immediate and unreserved respect when he demonstrated his skill at handling those two subversives. It had been nothing, really. A simple lesson in mechanics. The applying of all the muscles in the body in the turning over of a wrist. The pain that engendered in the owner of the wrist started instantaneous reflex action designed to relieve the pain, so that the lifting into the air and flopping over was done entirely by the muscles of the victim.

Its remarkableness was superficial. On the surface it probably had appeared to the uninitiated eye that he had lifted a man twice his weight and flopped him over on his back by brute force.

He smiled in the darkness. The horror of skulking death was gone now. For the moment, at least. Had the murderer realized his mistake? Was he even now searching? Edging between bodies as he looked for someone shorter than himself?

How would he find someone as short as—*him?* Henry visualized the murderer, touching one man after another, looking for a shoulder lower than others. Had there been another man as short as himself? Yes. He recalled that there had been another man in the group that was only five-feet-six or so.

The torture of claustrophobia rose to the surface of Henry's mind, driving away his calmness.

And then a light appeared forward.

By standing on tiptoe Henry could make it out. It was an illuminated sign reading, "No smoking. Fasten your seat belts."

A nervous laughter was drifting through the mass of densely packed flesh like a breeze rattling dry leaves on a tree in autumn. God Henry thought, how much warmth and comfort a little light can be to a man. He stayed on tiptoe, his eyes feasting on the light from the sign.

The touch of fingers on his shoulder was an electric alarm. His mind seemed to separate into two distinct parts, one controlling his movements, the other observing them.

He reached for and seized the fingers of the hand that had touched him. Even as he selected the middle finger of the hand and bent it with a backward twist until he felt it snap, broken, he marveled that such a plan for later identifying the man had formed in his mind without him being consciously aware of it.

As the finger broke under his pressure he let go of the hand; sensing its movement as it vanished. And already he was regretting his impulsive act. In all probability the person who had touched his shoulder was not the murderer but an innocent party. A badly needed worker would now be incapacitated for six weeks.

Oh well, Henry thought, grinning, the man would receive forty-two thousand dollars without working then.

The roar of the jets had died unnoticed. Now a shrill screaming whine rose as the plane dropped, braking with its wings as it went in for a landing. Henry felt himself squeezed forward as the plane decelerated.

Then a bump shook the floor. A moment later the rapid bumping of the floor told of the landing. It grew less and less. It stopped. They had arrived.

Abruptly the lights went on, blindingly.

SOMETHING jarred against the side of the ship. There were scraping metallic sounds. The hatch swung open.

"Move out, slowly," the metallic voice sounded. "Leave that body where it is. Step around it. When you get outside separate so that you're well spread out in the compound. Sit down and stay there. Get moving now. We haven't got all night."

With a shock Henry realized that it was night, here in Europe. It had been almost noon when they had left New York three hours ago.

The pressure of bodies ahead of him lessened. Joe and Al were on either side of him protectively. They ducked their heads and stepped out of the plane onto the ramp.

A landscape of fantasy met their eyes. A few miles away the widely spaced powerful lights began to merge, so that the horizon was a circle of incandescence. Above that rose a wide band of lights in a network of lines, rising tier upon tier. These lines could be nothing but the skeletal girders of the rising structure.

Half-stumbling down the ramp while he gazed in awe at the fantastic panorama of manmade landscape, Henry reached the bottom and stepped onto the floor. It was of metal. He looked down at it and wondered how far down the actual surface of the earth was. A hundred feet? A thousand?

"Move out and separate," a voice shouted, sounding feeble in the immensity of things.

"Over toward that gate," Al whispered. "Then nobody can pass us."

Henry looked in the direction Al had indicated. It was the exit to the enclosure. He nodded his agreement. It would be the ideal spot. He could be one of the first ones interviewed, and thus give the authorities what he knew of the murder so they could be on the watch for a man with a broken finger.

He reached a spot where he would be nearest the gates and sat down facing the plane. The last of the laborers came out and down the ramp.

For fifteen minutes there was no movement except for the moving around of uniformed soldiers, American soldiers. If there were any of the Lotissivians around they weren't in evidence.

Henry had never seen one in all the five years they had been here. He had of course seen innumerable pictures of them. They were definitely human, ranging in height from three feet to over five feet, with most of them just an inch or two over the three feet. Beautifully proportioned, they were like dolls.

The gates rattled open at Henry's back. He turned his head. A dozen soldiers with heavy service automatics at their hips were flanking three civilians. Henry recognized one of them as his chief, Major Winthrop.

Winthrop looked at him as he passed. Though there had been no sign of recognition, Henry was sure the major had recognized him. Now he would know that the murder was probably connected with the subversive movement, because he knew that Henry wouldn't have been on the plane unless suspected subversives were also on it.

The group went into the plane. A few minutes later Major Winthrop came out, flanked by two of the guards, and came back to the gate.

Workers under the directions of soldiers were now constructing a fenced-in lane from the compound to the building fifty yards away that appeared to be the airport offices. Trucks were lumbering up loaded with already constructed sections. Welders were tacking the sections to the metal floor. Twenty minutes saw the job done.

A uniformed officer strode down the fenced-in lane to the gate from the airport building.

"You," he said, pointing to Henry. "Come with me. The rest of you stay where you are. You'll be called one at a time."

Henry rose and followed the man. Shortly he was escorted into a room where Major Winthrop and several men in civilian clothes were standing. The officer who had brought him in left, closing the door behind him.

"Hello, Henry," Major Winthrop said calmly. "Make your report quickly and completely so that there will be no delay that might cast suspicion your way with the others of the load."

CHAPTER TWO

"...SO," HENRY said, summing up his report, "if the murdered man is my height the knife was intended for me, and if the man with a broken finger is one of those two, Paul Granch or Harry Lark, it makes it certain."

"We aren't too interested in the murder," Major Winthrop said. "I wish you hadn't broken the man's finger. It complicates things, not to mention putting a worker out of commission for it week or two. I don't believe you realize the full gravity of the situation, Henry."

"I think I do, sir," Henry said stiffly. "The Lotissivians will—"

"Yes, yes," the major cut in. "I know you are fully aware of *that* aspect of the situation. However, that isn't the major danger. In fact, it might be a good thing if the Lotissivians were to drop an occupation army and take over the United States. It's working very well in the other countries where it has been done, and all we are doing at present is running our government into bankruptcy in an effort to stall off the inevitable."

Henry Prince stared at the major, puzzled.

"If that isn't the thing we're trying to prevent," he said, "then you're right. I don't, as you say, realize the full gravity of the situation."

"The so-called subversives are the real focus of danger," the major said. "Do you see why?"

"They're the real threat?" Henry echoed, mystified. "But if you aren't worried about the Lotissivians taking over, how can the subversives be such a danger? All they can do is hamper recruiting of workers and get us so far behind schedule the Lotissivians will take over."

"If that were all we might even encourage them," Major Winthrop said. "But consider the overall picture."

"I don't know what you mean, Major Winthrop," Henry said. "I have considered the overall picture."

"The subversives are well organized," the major said slowly.

"I understand that, sir," Henry said.

"Who organized them?" the major shot out crisply. "Some group wanting the Lotissivians to occupy the one area they have left alone, the United States? If that were to happen, our financial structure would be dissolved and the system of benevolent slavery they have imposed on the rest of the world would be imposed. Who would gain by that?"

"I thought it was generally believed the subversives were a group of religious fanatics who think the Lotissivians are the hosts of the Lord, here to save mankind," Henry said doubtfully. "Surely there can't be any other explanation."

The major shook his head. "I didn't think you were that naive," he said. "You know a little of the number of the subversives. You know something of their ways of operating. That attempt to kill you, for example. Does that strike you as being the work of a religious group?"

"Then who?" Henry asked, a little of his exasperation creeping into his voice.

"We don't know," Major Winthrop said gravely. "But everything points toward it being some group intent on defying the Lotissivians themselves."

"What?" Henry said. "But that's absurd. It would be like a—a mosquito going lion hunting. They have several times the population of the Earth in spaceships circling the planet. They're invincible. Their science is as far beyond ours as ours is against that of the Seventeenth Century."

"Yes, yes," the major said. "It seems absurd. We would think it absurd. But there are two things that keep us from dismissing it as an absurdity. One, there is evidence of tremendous intelligence behind the subversives. Two, the Lotissivians seem afraid of something."

"Afraid?" Henry exclaimed. "Afraid when they stopped our world war cold in twenty-four hours, defeating the combined armed forces of both sides? Afraid when they occupy every portion of the globe with armies greater in numbers than the total population of the world, and could occupy the United States tomorrow as easily? And they have an estimated million and a quarter space battleships circling the Earth, each one able to lay waste to a thousand square miles by a flick of a Lotissivian's wrist, and come back and do it again to another thousand square miles, all day long?"

"Then why," the major said, emphasizing each word, *"don't* they occupy the United States? Why this giant building in the middle of what is left of Europe? *Why the necessity of having it completed by a certain date?* We can't answer any of those questions. But we're reasonably certain of two things. The Lotissivians, in spite of their might, are afraid to occupy the United States; and the subversives are *what* they are afraid of."

"I—I can't see it," Henry said. "I can't imagine what could possibly be a threat to them. Especially, anything originating on Earth. If there were another galactic horde as big as theirs within shooting distance of the Earth…"

"We don't know," Major Winthrop said. "We want to find out if we can. Therefore we're going to let this murder slide. We'll go through with our investigation of it, but make no arrests. And your orders are to try to make friends with Paul Granch and Harry Lark, and carry on in such a way that if they have any contacts you can get in touch with, you then become a subversive yourself."

"Yes, sir," Henry said.

"One more thing," the major said, "before you go back to the compound. I won't contact you again. If you make progress I'll see that you get cooperation. If you get orders to do some sabotage, or any other kind of orders, write them down and mail them to C.P.O.XXX. We'll see to it that you're a success as a traitor."

He smiled and held out his hand.

"WHY'D THEY take so long with you?" Joe said to Henry out of the corner of his mouth an hour later as the group was being led across the steel floor toward a distant line of portable shacks.

"They asked me to tell them all I remembered hearing when the guy was knifed," Henry said, shrugging indifferently. "So I told them."

"You tell them about those two punks?"

"Why should I?" Henry said.

"Yeah," Joe muttered. "That's right. But we're going to have trouble with them."

"Maybe," Henry said. He looked around and saw that the two, Paul and Harry weren't far behind. "What do you say we drop back and join them?"

Paul and Harry were pale and tight lipped as the three dropped into step beside them.

"See what I told you?" Henry said. "Where's the radioactivity? Aren't you glad you didn't back out now?"

"So what?" Paul Granch said nervously.

"So I was thinking the five of us might be better off sticking together," Henry said blandly. "With a murderer in the crowd he won't have a chance to knife any of us in the back if we stick together."

Henry turned his gaze to Harry Lark.

"What's the matter with you?" he asked.

His eyes dropped to where Harry's hand was hidden in a pocket.

"Nothing," Harry said. "Why don't you three punks scram? You ain't welcome here."

"Yeah?" Henry said. "Want a knife in your back like that other guy?"

"I suppose you're the one who knifed him?" Harry said.

"Shut up, Harry," Paul said.

"What's the matter with your hand, Harry?" Al asked innocently. "The way you hold it in your pocket looks funny, like it was hurt."

"Why don't you go peddle your papers before you get a knife in *your* back?" Harry gritted.

"My, my," Al said. "You don't learn your lessons very well, do you Harry?" He reached out quickly and tapped Harry's hand.

Harry cursed in a low voice thick with pain.

"Broken," Al muttered, surprised. He looked at Henry, his eyes wide and innocent. "Now I wonder who in this crowd knows how to break a finger quick and neat-like…"

"Why, Al," Henry said, "I was with you and Joe all the time on the plane."

"Names, please, gentlemen?"

It was a pleasant female voice. The line had stopped. The five men stared at the girl, startled. Joe recovered first.

"Mine's Joe," he said. "What's yours, honey?"

"That's it," the girl said. "Honey. Although some people prefer to call me sugar."

"No foolin'?" Joe said. "How's about a date my first day off from work, Honey?"

"Tell you what I'll do, Joe," Honey said, her tones intimate and promising. "I'll put you on my waiting list, and when your turn comes up I'll let you know."

"Waiting list?" Joe said, dismayed. He glanced doubtfully at the ledger book in her hands.

"Of course, Joe," she said. "Do you think there is *any* man in this line so discourteous as to neglect to ask me for a date?"

Her laughter was tinkling sleigh-bells, infectious.

Henry had been watching her quietly, taking in the almost golden richness of her hair under the pert hat, the saucy good nature that molded her features, the rich curves of her body that not even the sexless cut of her uniform could quite conceal.

Unconsciously he had stepped back so that the other four would be taken care of ahead of him.

"Your name?" she asked.

"Henry Prince," he said.

"Hen-ry...Prince," she wrote. Then she looked up at him expectantly while Joe, Al, Paul, and Harry waited.

Henry hesitated. He knew she was the nicest thing he had ever seen. He wanted desperately to get acquainted with her. But some instinct warned him that if he asked her for a date now she would strike him off as just another nice uninteresting male.

"Well?" Honey said sweetly.

"Oh, you're asking me for a date?" Henry said blandly. "I'm sorry, but with you tying up all the other males, I'll have to leave my free time open for other girls."

Was that a brief flash of disappointment he saw in her eyes? He couldn't be sure. But he had a sudden feeling that she was ready to put him at the top of her "list" right there.

"Your name?" she was saying to the next man...

THE NEXT morning after breakfast they were informed that the first day would be spent in a tour of the entire project.

By an adroit maneuver Paul and Harry managed to escape the company of Joe, Al, and Henry into a different group.

"Let them go for today," Henry said. "I want to talk with you two without them alone anyway."

Shortly they were speeding along the metal floor of the fabricated world they were now living in, in a sightseeing bus with transparent top. A skinny man standing at the front of the bus beside the driver spoke through a microphone into a loudspeaker.

He said, "This level we are on is the eight hundred foot level, the lowest still open. In most other areas the construction has already gone up to the nine hundred-foot level, and I understand that in about three weeks this area will be cleared for construction.

"The skeletal structure goes up four stories at a time, each story being twenty-five feet, and each area of construction being a mile square. Back home in the States, building a structure a hundred feet high covering a square mile of ground would be considered a major project. Here we have five thousand such separate projects in operation all the time. One hundred and eleven thousand of them have been completed. The schedule on each for a full crew is three months and eight days.

"The completed structure will have three hundred million tons of high tensile alumoy metal girders and plates in it, which, as you all know, is Russia's share in this work. There will be half a million miles of vertical elevator shafts carrying two million elevators, plus another half-million miles of horizontal shafts carrying two million cars.

"That should give you a rough idea of the size of the building you're going to be working on for the next two years…"

While the guide was talking, Henry, Joe, and Al had their heads together, talking in low voices.

"I've been wanting to find out how and why you broke Harry's finger," Al said impatiently.

"When we heard that scream of the man who was knifed," Henry explained, "I figured there might be a possibility of the killer learning it wasn't the right man. I knew he couldn't see, but only feel. Most of the men are six feet tall and I'm six inches shorter than most of them, so I figured if he continued looking for me sooner or later I would feel a hand touch my head or shoulder. So I stood on my toes to make myself taller, and waited. The minute I felt a hand touch my shoulder I grabbed it and broke a finger so I could know later who it was."

"Then Harry killed that fellow," Joe growled. "Did you tell them that when they had you in on the carpet?"

"It wouldn't be enough proof to convict a man," Henry hedged.

"You should have told about it anyway," Al said. "Those two know that you know who the killer is. They'll be after you all the more now. Sooner or later they'll get you."

"I wonder if they really did work for an organized group that was trying to scare off recruits for this job over here," Joe said. "If they were, we kind of upset their plans by making them sign up."

"Maybe," Henry said. "I think though that if the thing's that organized they probably have men right here trying all the time to sabotage construction. So Paul and Harry will go into that work, now that they're stuck here for two years the same way we are. I was thinking maybe by sticking close to them we might uncover the whole setup and really get something that will stick."

"Are you," Al asked dryly, "an undercover agent for the government, Hank? By any chance?"

"Oh sure," Henry grinned. "I signed up for this job just to get an extra thousand a day to augment my salary."

He studied the two men sharply, deciding from their grins at his remark that they were dismissing the possibility of him being a government agent from their thoughts.

"What I was thinking," Joe said seriously, "is that maybe they'll pass on the job of eliminating you—and maybe me and Al—to others in their organization. That way we wouldn't know what to guard against."

"Maybe," Henry admitted. "It's probably too late to do anything about that. But listen to my idea and see what you think of it. The subversives are probably plenty anxious to get recruits. And they probably pay good, too. What do you think of the idea of playing along with then, coming right out to Paul and Harry with a proposition to hook up with their gang, then breaking it up when we know where to do the breaking?"

"You talk awfully big," Joe said.

"How come you're still alive at—how old are you, Hank?" Al asked. "Twenty-four or so?"

Henry grinned and turned his head toward the window of the bus, not pressing the point. He knew he would get an answer only after the two men had talked it over between themselves, and that nothing more he could say at present would help.

CHAPTER THREE

"THINK I'll try my luck with Honey once more," Joe said, standing up and stretching casually.

Henry glanced briefly at him and nodded with apparent disinterest. Joe and Al had been whispering together off and on. He knew they had been discussing his proposition. This could have something to do with that, or it could be just what it seemed.

Paul and Harry, sitting together within earshot, seemed not to have been listening.

Joe walked down the aisle between the rows of cots toward the exit. When the door closed on him, Paul rose and started out. Instantly Al, who had seemed half-asleep, rose to his feet and caught up with him.

"Go back and sit down," he said. "You ain't going anyplace."

He stood there belligerently until Paul had returned to his cot, then went slowly back to Henry.

"Imagine," he drawled. "Paul doesn't even want Joe to make time with a good-looking girl."

Outside, Joe went to a building that had been pointed out as the women's dormitory. He hesitated briefly, then entered, finding himself in a hall that served as lobby. He felt more at ease when he saw here and there a man sitting with a girl, talking. He crossed the lobby to the desk.

"Yes?" the capable-looking woman behind the counter asked.

"I want to speak to Honey," Joe said uncomfortably. "I don't know her last name. She's the one who took our names yesterday."

"You must mean Honey Childs," the woman said. "I'll ring her room and ask her if she'll see you. What's your name?"

A moment later the woman looked up from the phone with an apologetic expression on her face.

"I'm very sorry," she said, "but Honey has a headache and can't come down."

"Wait a minute," Joe said hastily. "Don't hang up yet. Tell her I'm not trying to date her. I've got to talk to her about something very important."

The woman hesitated, then repeated Joe's words into the phone. She hung up and came to the counter.

"Sit over there," she said, pointing to a chair. "She'll be down in a moment."

Joe smiled his thanks and went over and sat down. It was nearly ten minutes before Honey appeared. Joe felt an inner thrill as her eyes lit up with recognition. She came over and sat down in a chair facing him.

"I'm sorry, Joe," she said. "I didn't know who it was, and so many of the new recruits try to date me that it gets monotonous, though I try to keep remembering that each one is a sincere human being."

"Yeah," Joe said, finding his tongue thick and clumsy. "That's all right. I wouldn't have bothered you for myself."

"Then it's Henry Prince?" she said eagerly.

"Well..." Joe hesitated. Suddenly he leaned forward. "I won't beat around the bush. I don't know how well acquainted you are around here, but I've got to talk to somebody in charge of things. The big boss, or something. It's very important. I don't want to tell you what it's about, because I don't want you in any danger."

"Danger?" Honey Childs said. "What are you talking about?" She studied Joe closely, then seemed to make up her mind. "All right, Joe," she said. "I won't ask any questions."

She stood up and went over to a row of phone booths. On her way back she stopped at the desk and whispered with the woman there. Joe saw the woman nod and glance over at him. Then Honey came back and sat down.

"There are small cars here for couples to go riding in," she said. "In a minute we'll go out just like we were going riding together, which we'll actually do. I'll do the driving and—" she smiled impudently—"no monkey business."

"Who, me?" Joe said.

Honey looked at him, then impulsively reached out and placed her hand over his.

"Or at least not much monkey business," she added, jerking back as she saw the happy look in his eyes.

SHE DROVE through the city of housing quarters, her attention concentrated on the way ahead, while Joe sat beside her, his mission all but forgotten in the spell of her presence.

The housing section was soon left behind. Ahead stretched miles of almost mathematically flat expanse vanishing into the horizon of overhead lighting in the distance.

In fifteen minutes a high cliff of exposed girders loomed ahead. Honey didn't slow down. At the last moment an opening appeared through the lights. Then the car was speeding through a long tunnel.

Suddenly she braked sharply, turning into what appeared to be a two-car garage, and stopping. She honked the horn. Joe felt himself sink deeper into the seat under the force of upward acceleration, and realized that they were on an elevator.

When it came to a stop Honey started the car again.

"You're awfully quiet," she said, flashing him a smile. "I thought I was going to have to fight you off when we were in the elevator, and you didn't even look at me."

"I thought of it," Joe confessed. "But you're too high class for me. You're more Henry's type. I'm just a common lug."

Honey drove in silence, a twisted smile on her red velvet lips. Joe looked out the window at the tunnel walls speeding by.

"Yeah" Honey said, aping his melancholy. "I guess you're right. I'm more Henry's type. High class."

Joe frowned at her suspiciously but she stared straight ahead at the roadway. When he turned his eyes back to the road she slowly exhaled the breath she had been holding.

Numbers appeared on the roadway ahead. Honey slowed the car, turned into another tunnel, pulled over to the outer lane and stopped the car beside a platform.

"They're waiting for you," she said, quietly.

Joe opened the door and started to get out. Suddenly he turned and faced her.

"Honey," he said.

"Yes?"

"Uh," he said uncomfortably, "thanks for helping me this way." He backed out of the door.

"Don't mention it," Honey said, her eyes flashing in sudden anger.

"Now I wonder what I did to make her mad?" Joe muttered as he hurried across the platform.

"JOSEPH WRIGHT?" the man said. "I'm Major Winthrop. Miss Childs said you had something very important to report."

"Yes, sir," Joe said. "Al and I talked it over and decided we'd better let somebody know. It's about Henry's idea. He wants to get in with the fellows trying to sabotage operations."

"I'm glad you decided to report it," the major said. "That's very serious. He could be shot for trying to do a thing like that."

"That's not it, exactly," Joe said. "He thinks we could get in with them and learn all about them, and maybe get a fat reward for breaking the whole thing up."

"What did you say his name was?" Major Winthrop asked sharply.

"Henry Prince," Joe said uncomfortably. "This won't get him in trouble? He's not a traitor. He's very patriotic."

"Who are these men he wants to get in with?" the major asked.

"I'd rather not say just now, sir," Joe said. "Henry wouldn't like that. He thinks we should handle it alone."

"Does it have anything to do with that murder on the plane?" the major asked.

"It might," Joe hedged.

Major Winthrop appeared to be thinking. He listened while Joe continued a halting explanation of what they were planning to do.

"Might be a good idea," the major said finally. "I'm glad you came to me, though. Now here's what I want you to do, you and your friend Al. I want you to keep me informed of your activities. Don't tell Henry Prince about this though. Let him keep thinking you're playing along with his plans.

"But you'll need cooperation from us sometimes, especially if you make a definite contact and get assignments to do any dirty work. We could stand a little sabotage if the end result is getting at the root of the whole business. So go along with Prince, and if at any time something comes up that we should know about so your plans won't get you involved in trouble, write a brief note and address it simply to C.P.O.XXX. Drop it in a mailbox. We'll get it in a few hours."

"Yes sir," Joe said. "C.P.O.XXX. What does that triple X stand for?"

"That's just an identifying set of letters," the major said. He smiled disarmingly and shook hands with Joe in dismissal.

Back in the car Joe relaxed with a happy sigh.

"Everything all right?" Honey asked, turning the car.

"Better than I expected," Joe said.

"What about your friends?" Honey said. "Won't they suspect something?"

"I—I told them I was going to try to date you," Joe said.

"Well," Honey said, her eyes straight ahead. "I guess you can tell them you did without telling a lie. We went for a ride, didn't we? Still—" she frowned in apparent study of the problem—"they might not believe you. Of course, you could kiss me. That would leave some lipstick on you..."

"Yeah," Joe said. "I could sort of forget I had it on. Then I could pretend to be surprised when they saw it on me. But would you...I mean, it would be a lot to ask you to do..."

Honey stopped the car, leaving the motor running. Then she turned to Joe.

"I—*I'm* willing, Joe," she said. She lifted her head and closed her eyes.

Joe looked at her pale inviting features for an instant, then his arms crept about her slim waist and he kissed her. He drew her closer, feeling her yield. Then suddenly he drew away from her.

"What about Hank?" he said. "This'll queer things between you and him."

"Oh forget about Hank," Honey said sharply.

Her expression softened, a dreamy, almost hypnotic, quality creeping into her eyes. Joe leaned forward slowly, watching her eyes close in expectation, feeling her lips meet his, her body curve under the pressure of his embrace.

"Joe..." she said drowsily.

"Yeah, Honey," Joe murmured.

"What was that all about that you came here to see the major for?"

"I'd better not tell you," he said. "It would be too dangerous for you to know anything."

"You mean you don't trust me?" she asked, leaning back and looking at him with round eyes.

"No, of course I don't mean that," he said gently. "I mean it would be dangerous for you. It has to do with a subversive group trying to sabotage construction that we're going to try to uncover."

"But I might just as well know," Honey said. "If they know you're out to get them they'll know I was with you and I'll be in danger anyway."

"Gee," Joe said, straightening. "I never thought of that. Here I've been stupid enough to place you in danger and that's the last thing I wanted to do."

"Well it's too late to be sorry about it," Honey said. "I might as well know everything. Then I can recognize danger when I see it, and maybe even be able to help out."

She pushed Joe away from her and got behind the wheel.

"I know a good place to park while we talk," she said, starting the car. "It's called Lovers' Leap…"

HENRY PRINCE watched Joe through slitted eyes, pretending to be asleep. He felt Joe's eyes on him briefly, passing to Al's cot. He saw Joe touch Al's foot, heard the deep breathing of the sleeping man stop abruptly, saw Joe's expressionless nod. He didn't move when Joe climbed into the cot next to his. After that he lay awake for a long time…

A bell was clanging jarringly. Everybody was stirring. Henry sat up. Al was already sitting at the foot of his cot getting dressed. Joe groaned protestingly and sat up.

"What's that on your face, Joe?" Al asked.

Henry looked. It was red, smeared almost lavishly. Lipstick. He went cold inside. When he tried to match Al's delighted laughter his grin was sickly. Joe was trying to wipe it off.

"I forgot it might show," Joe was saying disgustedly.

"Well, congratulations, Joe," Henry said, shrugging off the feeling of loss. "She's a nice girl."

"Ah, she's just a dame," Joe said, but his indifference was less than skin deep.

They were dressing now.

"We went for a ride," Joe went on. "Drove clear over to the edge where we could look down on the Danube. The river's packed with big cargo boats. Bringing girders and plates from Russia, I guess. They looked small from nine hundred feet up."

"Where'd you get the car?" Al asked.

"Oh, she got it," Joe said.

"See you in the washroom," Henry said, picking up his travel case and towel, and hurrying away without waiting for an answer.

A few moments later Joe and Al joined him.

"About that scheme of yours," Al said, "we've decided to play along. Make it a partnership. Share the risk and share equally on any reward."

"It's a deal," Henry said. "Now we've got to corner Paul and Harry and put it up to them. Convince them we want to tie in with them."

"Right," Al said.

But it seemed the opportunity wouldn't come soon. Paul and Harry managed to eat at another table. They ate hurriedly and slipped out during a moment when none of the three was watching.

"Guess it'll have to be tonight," Joe grumbled.

The three finished their breakfast glumly, then rose and went to the exit.

"Your names?" a man just outside the door said. They told him and he looked over a list, took three cards from a small file box and handed them over. "Give these to a man standing by a truck with the number three painted on its side. The truck'll take you where you're supposed to work."

Paul and Harry were standing beside the truck. Their faces darkened when they saw them approach.

"Looks like we're going to be working in the same spot," Joe said to them, grinning.

"Come here, you two," Al said inaudibly. "We want to make a deal with you."

Paul and Harry's eyes widened in surprise. They followed the three to a spot where they wouldn't be overheard.

"What's the deal?" Harry asked.

"You been wondering why Hank didn't tip off the authorities about you two punks?" Al said. "He had a reason. I've had a reason. We ain't satisfied with what we'll have left of the thousand a day after taxes. We knew you must be hooked up with some organization that has plenty of dough, because sabotage don't come cheap. We want in on it."

Paul and Harry looked at each other, their expressions unreadable.

"You got us wrong," Paul said stiffly. "We ain't hooked up with nobody in anything like that."

"Suit yourself." Al shrugged. "Too bad you ain't. It would fix things up nice between us. We could be pals, instead of each of us wondering what accident was going to happen next that might be worse than a busted finger. In fact, I got a hunch something might happen right today. People who know too much to live, generally don't—very long."

"Suppose we did have—connections," Harry said, nursing his broken finger, now in a plaster cast. "Just supposing, don't you think it would be much easier just to have you three meet with a fatal accident than let you live with what you think you know?"

"Not the way I see it," Al said. "I think they need men. Good men. Not bungling punks. I dare you to pass the word along to them that we want to hook up. They'd probably get rid of you two before the day's out and contact us themselves."

"Come on," Henry said. "We're wasting our time. Who'd be dumb enough to trust anything to these two?"

"Yeah," Joe growled. "Take a last look at them, because they probably won't be alive, come lunch time."

Joe, Al, and Henry grinned sinisterly and turned their backs, going to the truck. After they were in they looked over to see what Paul and Harry were doing. They were no place in sight at the moment.

"What the—where could they have run to?" Al said.

"Maybe their contact is around close," Henry said. "It could be they've gone to ask about us. If that's so, we'll be hearing about it quick, because Paul and Harry won't like the idea of dying before lunch time." They chuckled softly, the chuckle of men who know they themselves might not be alive much longer.

THE TRUCK began to fill with men. At the last moment before starting, Paul and Harry climbed on.

"It's a truce for the present," Paul mumbled near Henry's ear. "I'm not saying anything, but maybe, just maybe, you'll get something definite that'll fix things between all of us."

"Okay, a truce," Henry said. "But you don't mind if we don't trust you just yet, do you?"

Paul went on toward the front of the truck with Harry. Henry told his companions what Paul had said.

"Looks like he meant someone will contact us," Al said. "They'd have to. We can't afford to take any say-so from them two. Wonder who it will be?"

"Maybe nobody," Henry said. "They might not chance letting us see them. My guess is it will be a note for us to be at a certain place tonight. Then it will depend on whether they need us if we get the works or a proposition."

The truck started moving. Other trucks were in the line ahead and behind, going toward the hundred-foot wall that hid the construction work they were being taken to.

Shortly the string of trucks entered a tunnel. After a short distance they turned onto an area that held ten trucks at once. As the last truck pulled into position the whole thing began to rise. It was an elevator.

Henry reached into his pocket for a cigarette, his eyes looking downward toward his knees absently. Suddenly a small folded piece of paper seemed to materialize a few inches above his lap, poise there for a second, then drop. He glanced up quickly, looking around. No one was paying any attention to him.

He thought, "Of course it was a trick of my eyes. Someone threw it."

He picked it up and unfolded it casually. Joe and Al noticed it and leaned over to read it with him. It read:

Mr. Prince: You and your two companions will be at the rear of the building in which you sleep at precisely ten-thirty this evening and stand at least ten feet away from the wall of the building in plain sight.

"Where'd that come from?" Joe asked.

"I don't know," Henry said. "It seemed to materialize right in front of me."

"I don't see how," Joe said uneasily. "I've had my eyes on those two, and they haven't written anything. They couldn't write like that, anyway."

"No, they couldn't," Henry admitted. "This was written by someone who has made an art of penmanship. It was written carefully at a desk, not scribbled in someone's lap on a moving truck."

"Anyway this is it," Al said. "Tonight we get knocked off or get a new job."

The trucks were moving again. They didn't go far, parking with their noses against a platform, which stretched out a hundred yards, dotted with all types of benches and machines.

They were ordered to line up and a man with a pile of cards started calling off their names. As each man called stepped forward he was told where to go in a definite tone.

Henry found himself at a bench on which lay several thick pieces of metal with beveled edges, and a device on small wheels, which he knew must be some type of machine welder.

He occupied his time studying the machine without touching it, figuring out its probable behavior. After a while an instructor came around and showed him how to operate it, giving him a booklet of instructions. From the booklet he learned that all girders and plates were to be welded rather than riveted, and that his future job would be welding joints.

"THINK I'll write the folks back home," Joe said. "I'll see you guys at supper."

"I'll join you," Henry said quickly. "I've got to drop a line to a friend."

Joe hesitated, then fell in beside Henry, who smiled slightly to himself, having guessed that Major Winthrop had probably instructed Joe to keep making reports to him through the XXX address. It was a wise precaution, because at any time it might become impossible for Henry to make them. Then Joe's report would suffice.

Fifteen minutes later they dropped their envelopes in the mailbox in the reading room, each being casually careful that the address on the envelope didn't show.

"Well," Joe said, glancing at his watch, "six-thirty. Four more hours."

"Hope they have something good to eat," Henry said.

"Yeah," Joe grunted. "Condemned men..."

At twenty after ten Joe, Al, and Henry casually pushed back from the table where they had been playing three-handed pinochle and strolled toward the door. Paul and Harry, over in one corner of the room, followed them with their eyes.

Outside the building the overhead lights made every square foot of the flat metal terrain light as day. The three stood idly in front of the building talking small talk, then slowly strolled to the space between their building and the next.

At ten-twenty-nine they reached the rear of the building and paused ten feet out from it, casually half turning their backs to one another so that they could command a view in all directions, even glancing upward into the clear sky to be sure there was nothing that could drop on them from above.

"I see you obeyed orders," a voice said.

They whirled in the direction of the voice. Standing among them was a figure shaped vaguely like a man. There had been no way he could have approached without being seen, yet he was there.

"What the—" Joe gasped.

"Surprised?" the figure said mildly. "I don't blame you. I always enjoy the expression on the face of a newcomer to our ranks. You wonder how I got here? I materialized." The figure vanished for a moment, then appeared again. "See?" it said calmly. "Now stay close together so that if anyone's looking they won't notice me. My shape is rather—ah—unusual. It would attract attention."

"It isn't your shape so much," Joe said. "It's your face. You look like the devil. Literally."

"Thank you, thank you," it said. "But my shape is as normal to me as yours is to you. In my race of humans we run to points instead of curves. Pointed ears, pointed chin." The voice changed abruptly, becoming business-like. "I understand you wish to join your countrymen who are working to—ah, shall we say—further the Cause?"

"After seeing you, I wonder," Joe said. "You make me think of stories of people selling their souls to the devil."

"All superstition has a basis in fact," the being said, "including that one. However, we aren't in league with the mythical being called the devil. We are a perfectly legitimate offshoot of the human race, just as real as you."

"Just what is this Cause?" Henry spoke up. "I thought it was just some underground organization headed by a group with plenty of money and a desire to try either to drive the Lotissivians away or make them drop an occupation force into the U.S. After seeing you I don't know what to think."

"I'll explain," the being said crisply. "You see, we were getting along very nicely before the Lotissivians arrived. If they stay it will complicate things considerably. They are a uni-planar civilization just like your own, though much more advanced. Hyper-blind-mutes, and even to a large extent hyper-deaf.

"They've conquered your civilization, but not ours. We alone can fight them successfully, because their weapons can't touch us.

"But I've stayed here too long. I came only to convince you that there is something to work for. You will be amply rewarded, and I might add, not at the expense of selling your souls. From time to time you will receive specific orders, and we will expect them carried out to the letter. Here." He handed each of them a small coin-shaped object. "When you wish to summon me or one of my fellow beings, hold this in your hand. The warmth of your hand will activate it."

Suddenly the being was not there.

"NOT AT the expense of selling our souls," Al muttered. "I wish I had gone to church more often."

The being appeared again suddenly.

"Will you please drop your *charrymns* in your pockets," it said impatiently. It waited while they did so in guilty haste. "Thank you," it said, and was gone.

"I wonder if the thing can hear us when it isn't here," Joe muttered uneasily.

"I don't think so," Henry said. "Otherwise why would we need these charms, as it called these things it gave us?"

"Well," Joe said. "Looks like we're in. How do we get *out?*"

"That is a question," Henry said dryly. "We thought all we would run into were some people that could be captured. How do you capture something that isn't human, and can vanish right before your eyes?"

"I think there are ways," Joe said. "I remember hearing about some book on black magic that tells how to capture an evil spirit. If this thing isn't a spirit or a devil, I'll eat my hat."

"I think we've gotten into something we won't get out of," Al said. "But now I can see a whole lot I would never have guessed. Assuming Heaven and Hell exist, or some counterpart of them that could accommodate what we just met, the coming of the Lotissivians would upset the whole business. But that thing certainly wasn't a spirit of any kind. It was solid. As solid as this charm in my pocket."

"That's no lie," Joe agreed. "But there's nothing to be gained by standing out here. Let's go to bed. We know how Paul and Harry got in touch with their boss now. They must have charms like ours."

The three strolled casually around to the front of the building and entered.

"Guess I'll go in and read for a while," Joe said carelessly. "You guys go on to bed."

"O.K.," Henry said, smiling to himself. He knew Joe was going to make a report and mail it. There would be no necessity for two reports now.

He and Al went on into the sleeping room to their cots. There Henry dumped the *charrymn* out of his pocket onto the blanket and examined it without touching it.

It was the size of a half-dollar and slightly thicker, of gold or some similar metal. It appeared to have been stamped like a coin.

He leaned forward to examine the design more closely. The figure on it was of a man standing upright with arms raised outward and legs spread apart. There was fine writing around the perimeter. It was in the same fine hand as the script on the note that had appeared out of nowhere and fallen in to his lap.

That note! Then it *had* appeared out of nowhere. That being or one of his kind had been in the truck and dropped it in his lap.

He thought of what the major had said about the Lotissivians being afraid to occupy the United States. That was understandable now. That being hadn't been a sprit or a devil, but a purely material, living being of some kind. It had come from nowhere in the space of three dimensions. It had spoken of hyper-blindness, and hyper was a prefix used to express four-dimensionalness. So there must be a place in some other three-dimensional space connected with the ordinary one where there were large numbers of these things with pointed ears and chins.

The Lotissivians must know about them, maybe even having instruments to *see* into their dimension, and this extra-spatial race must have a large concentration in the United States but nowhere else, since the Lotissivians had landed in other areas with impunity.

Henry undressed slowly, looking at the *charrymn*, finally turning it over with his thumbnail and studying the other side. He decided it must be some very delicate device disguised as a coin. Under its surface must be some complex circuit or device able to send a signal into the fourth dimension. American scientists would give much to be able to dissect that coin and discover the principle of its operation. But would the being come and snatch it from under their noses if he sent it to the major? And what would happen to him if that thing ever suspected him of being connected with the government?

Perhaps even now it was bending over Joe's shoulder, reading his report. It might do nothing, allowing him to mail it. Perhaps it could take the letter out of the mailbox through the fourth dimension...

He stretched out in bed. When Joe came in he sighed with relief and closed his eyes.

CHAPTER FOUR

"WHAT'RE you dressing up for, Joe?" Al asked.

"Got a date," Joe said, winking broadly.

Henry turned away, hiding the bleakness that came to his face. He wished now that he had asked Honey Childs for a date that first day. She might have accepted. Now it was too late. He couldn't very well try to horn in on Joe's girl.

Joe departed, but was back in a few moments.

"Forgot something," he said.

He cautiously slipped the *charrymn* out of his work clothes into the pocket of his suit and left again.

And shortly he was seated beside Honey in a car once more, speeding toward the now familiar tube into the section where he had gone with her on that other ride, and in which he had been working during the four days since then.

"We're in," Joe said. "I don't think I like it, but we're in. We met one of the bosses of the underground, *and is it an underground.* In more than one sense of the word."

"Save it, Joe," Honey said. "Wait until we're parked."

"This won't wait," Joe said, slipping his arm around her and cupping her chin in his huge hand.

Her lips yielded to his for a long moment. She pulled away.

"Darn you, Joe," she said. "Now I've lost the white line."

"To the left, I think, Honey."

Honey found the guideline again and stopped the car.

"Take your kiss back," she said, "and save it until we reach Lover's Leap."

Joe was very sober when the car started again. Honey glanced at him from time to time, studying him. She turned the car onto the elevator and honked the horn.

"Why so sober, Joe?" she asked.

"I was just thinking," Joe said. "You're a high class girl. Educated. Rich parents. I'm' nothing. Just a punk. I guess I've sort of taken advantage of you, your loneliness. When we get back to the states it wouldn't be any good. I wouldn't know how to act. Even this suit I have on feels uncomfortable."

"I'll tell you something, Joe," Honey said softly. "I was just kidding you. I'm from southern Illinois, a small town. My dad's a grocer. I—I always wanted to fall in love with a big bruiser with the heart of a baby. I—I sort of guess maybe I have."

"Then it was me all the time, and not Henry?" Joe asked, his voice choked.

"Since the first," Honey said. "I wouldn't have dated him if he'd asked. I guess I shouldn't say it, but I kept hoping you would try again."

"Gee," Joe said. He reached out a huge paw and patted her clumsily on the cheek.

They became aware at the same time that the elevator had stopped some time before; looked at each other, laughing in embarrassment.

HONEY started the car, driving in silence until she stopped at the spot where they had parked that first night.

"Now," she said. "Tell me all about what happened."

She settled in his arms while he talked. When he told about the being who had suddenly appeared she pulled away, her eyes wide in the gloom.

"Describe him," she said queerly. "Every detail that you can remember."

She drew in her breath sharply when he told about the coin.

"A charm?" she asked. "Are you sure he called it that?"

"It sounded something like that," Joe said, "but now that you mention it, maybe he pronounced it funny. He put an extra sound in it, kind of stretching out the R."

"Like *charrymn?*" Honey asked.

"Yeah!" Joe said. "That's the way he said it. I've got it with me but I'm afraid to take it out of my pocket. Holding it in your hand sets up some kind of signal that makes the guy with the pointed ears appear."

"Oh let's not talk about it any more," Honey said huskily, lifting her face and veiling her eyes dreamily with olive lids...

Three hours later he entered the darkened hall where one hundred and forty-nine men lay sleeping. He was whistling under his breath. When he sat down at the end of his cot the creaking awakened Henry.

Henry opened his eyes and watched Joe without moving. He saw him take off his coat and feel in a pocket. The softly whistled melody stopped abruptly. Joe's hands searched pocket after pocket swiftly. Then Joe cursed softly, dressing again hurriedly.

He was gone a half-hour. When he returned he undressed again, and stretched out on his cot with a deep sigh.

Henry lay wide awake. From Joe's actions it was obvious he had lost the coin-shaped device. Henry wondered how he had lost it, what would come of it. Had the thing been stolen from Joe's pocket? Or had it merely slipped out, so that someone would find it and pick it up? If that happened, whoever found it would be in for a distinct shock.

Or had Honey taken it? It was fairly certain that it was she who had taken Joe to Major Winthrop. It was likely she had coaxed Joe to take her into his confidence. A girl like her could have just about anyone she wanted, so why should she settle for Joe? Was there some ulterior reason? Henry pondered this possibility. She certainly wasn't connected with any secret government organization or he would have been informed of the fact—or would he? Why would she steal the coin?

"WHAT'S the matter with you, Joe?" Al asked good-naturedly. "Did Honey give you the brush-off last night?"

Joe, lacing his shoes, shook his head but didn't look up.

"Something's eatin' you," Al said.

"So what?" Joe growled. "Shut up and mind your own business."

Al took a quickstep toward Joe and gave him a rabbit punch that carried him off the bed face down on the floor. The room became suddenly hushed.

Joe rose in a half crouch.

"Al's in the right, Joe," Henry said softly. "Tell us what's wrong or I'll take you apart myself."

Joe switched his glare from Al to Henry, then the mad light in his eyes died down.

"I guess you're right," he mumbled. "Come on. Let's go wash up and I'll tell you."

He stood up and casually put his hands in his pockets. A ludicrous expression appeared on his features. It vanished quickly, leaving his face calm. But his eyes were shrewd and thoughtful.

"Last night I put that coin in my coat pocket when I went out," he said when they were in the washroom. "When I got back it was gone. I thought I lost it. I looked in every pocket I own. It wasn't in any of them. Now, this morning, it's in my work trousers..."

"Is it the same one?" Henry asked.

Joe took his handkerchief and used it to bring the *charrymn* out of his pocket. They examined it. So far as they could tell it was the same.

"The only explanation is that you were mistaken," Al said. "How could it get lost and then show up in your pocket?"

"I wonder," Henry said thoughtfully. "Suppose he lost it and someone found it. They'd hold it in their hand and look at it. That whatever-it-is would appear, realize the guy wasn't the one who was supposed to have it, maybe take it away from him while he stood there with his mouth open wondering what it was all about, and return it to Joe."

"Yes, that must be the way it happened," Joe said eagerly. "Sure. Why didn't I think of it?"

They went to the dining room. There was an excited buzzing of conversation around the tables. When they sat down they learned what it was about.

"Did you hear about the monster they found outside this morning?" someone asked them. Taking their blank looks as an answer he went on, "Dead. Right in the middle of the street. It's the size of a human being and shaped a lot like one, but it has long ears pointed at the top, a chin that comes to a sharp point, and a bright red skin."

"Dead?" Henry said. "What killed it?"

"I didn't hear," the man said. "I went outside to look, but they'd already taken the thing away."

Henry, Joe and Al looked at each other uneasily.

"It could be connected with your losing that charm," Al mumbled.

"They aren't called charms," Joe said. "They're called *charrymns.*"

"Where'd you learn that?" Henry asked sharply.

"Honey," Joe said. Then he looked puzzled. "But how did she know?" He shrugged. "I guess she didn't."

"You mean you've been telling her all about this, you dumb fool?" Al asked angrily. "Good grief Joe, how stupid can you get?"

Joe flushed at having given himself away. This was something he hadn't told Al.

"Did you show her the *charrymn?*" Henry broke in.

"No," Joe said. "She didn't ask to see it."

"Then she knew what it looked like," Al said. "That dame's too mixed up in this. I'll bet she stole it out of your pocket, Joe."

Something at the front of the dining room was attracting everyone's attention. Henry, Joe and Al looked to see what it was. There were four men in M.P. uniforms. They were coming toward them, glancing briefly at each face as though looking for someone.

"I've got a hunch," Henry said quickly. "Quick, Joe, give me that *charrymn.*"

The four M.P.'s were now coming toward them purposefully. They stopped beside Joe.

"You the one who was out with Miss Childs last night?" one of them asked.

"Yeah," Joe said. "Is anything wrong?"

"Come with us," the M.P. said.

HENRY looked at the grim expressions on the M.P.'s faces, saw the troubled uneasiness of Joe's manner. He wondered if Joe had told everything.

"Am I under arrest or something?" Joe asked.

"We have orders to bring you in," the spokesman for the M.P.'s said. "Whether they lock you up or just question you makes no difference. Are you coming peaceably?"

Joe nodded.

Henry and Al watched him depart with the officers.

"That was a lucky hunch of yours to take his *charrymn*," Al said. "Say... You know, that's the way that fellow pronounced it. I wonder how Honey knew that. She doesn't seem the type that would be tied in with those things with pointed ears."

"I have another hunch," Henry said. "They asked Joe if he was the one who was out with Honey last night. They took him in for questioning. That adds up to Honey Childs having disappeared."

"What?" Al exclaimed. "Say, you may be right at that. If she swiped that thing from Joe and got to monkeying with it, and old Pointed Ears appeared, he might have taken her with him to shut her up."

"The only thing I can't figure," Henry said, "is that dead one. Honey couldn't have killed one of those fellows."

"Maybe there was more than one of them," Al said. "They must have kidnapped her. Maybe that one was killed by the military police."

"I don't know," Henry said. "I keep having a strange feeling that there's even more to this than we think. If Joe comes back we can find out more about what happened. Until then we might as well forget about it."

"Yeah, let's eat our breakfast," Al said.

Joe didn't return. Al and Henry waited until the last minute to board the trucks that would take them to their work.

"Guess it must be serious," Al muttered. "Maybe we should conjure up that devil and ask him what's going on. What do you think, Hank?"

"I was just thinking the same thing," Henry said. "If Joe isn't back by tonight I'm for it, even though I hate the idea of seeing that thing again. I wonder if the dead one was the one we met?"

Henry decided by the middle of the afternoon that it was the longest day he had ever experienced. He was now a welder, working often alone. But today he wasn't alone. There was no chance to summon up the "devil", as Al had dubbed it. Not only was he working with a crew, but also every few minutes someone would come around to ask questions about Joe's being taken by the M.P.'s.

He wished they would leave him alone. He became curt with those working around him when they talked to him. Then suddenly he realized the true cause of his irritation was not the men around him but something else.

The moment he realized this he was able to isolate it. It was a strange tingling, almost an electric shock, that seeped through him each time his machine welder was operating. It seemed to originate near his right hip.

He thought of the *charrymn* and wondered if that could be acting up. But it hadn't done so before. Memory of having taken Joe's when the M.P.'s were coming flashed into his thoughts. So that was it...

They had some strange power, perhaps very weak; but when there were two of them together their combined power affected the nervous system. He quickly transferred one of them to the left pocket of his trousers.

The relief was immediate. The irritating waves stopped.

The welder was set up for a run.

He stooped over, absently reaching for the toggle switch. He missed it, and automatically brought his eyes to it to guide his finger. What he saw sent a tingling shock through him. His finger was half buried in the switchbox.

Instinctively he jerked it away, and saw it pull out of the solidity of the machine unharmed. Puzzled, he brought his finger against the toggle arm, feeling it touch lightly. He pushed—and his finger passed through the solid plastic.

A fear greater than any he had ever experienced took hold. Trembling, he reached into his left pocket, hoping that his fingers would be able to hold the *charrymn* he had just placed there. It was solid to his fingers. He took it out and put it back with the other one.

He looked around. No one was paying any attention to him. They had noticed nothing. Had there really been anything for them to notice? The sight of his finger half buried in solid matter rose before his eyes. The fear returned. It rose from some deep corner of his mind that believed in black magic and voodoo spirits. He trembled almost visibly, not able to quiet himself. And waves of torture crept from the two *charrymns* into his hip.

"WHAT'S THE matter with you, Hank?" Al asked as they met at the trucks at quitting time.

"Nothing," Henry said. "Shut up—and for God's sake stick close to me."

Half an hour later when the truck stopped in front of the dorm building they hurried inside to see if Joe had returned yet. He hadn't.

Henry left Al and went into the reading room. He scribbled a hasty note: "Must see you immediately. Vitally important." He addressed the envelope to C.P.O.XXX and dropped it in the box, then rejoined Al.

"How about letting me in on what's eating you?" Al asked.

"I don't know myself," Henry said. "I wish I did."

They joined the drift into the dining room. A fit of trembling possessed Henry. Al gripped his shoulder, sympathy in his eyes.

"Thanks," Henry mumbled. He felt the trembling gradually subside.

They had nearly finished eating when the same four M.P.'s that had come for Joe in the morning came into the dining room. Henry breathed a soft sigh of relief.

"Are they coming for you or me?" Al muttered. "What'll we do about the *charrymns?*"

"Probably you," Henry said. "Give yours to me."

He regretted his impulse. If two of the mysterious things did so much to him, three would be infinitely worse. But some corner of his mind seemed to have taken over his will. He felt Al's hand thrust a napkin wrapped small object in his hand. He wrapped the napkin around it more completely and slipped it into his pocket with the other two. Now he had all three.

The M.P.'s stopped by them. "Are you Henry Prince?" one of them asked. As he nodded, "Come with us please."

Henry stood up slowly, pretending surprise. He looked toward Al with what he hoped was questioning helplessness, then went with the M.P.'s.

As he followed the guards to their car and it sped toward its destination, Henry tried to pin down the cause of his fear. There was so much he didn't know, so much he knew that didn't make sense at all. The red beings and their ability to materialize and dematerialize at will. The flat statement the "devil" had made that the Lotissivians couldn't reach them. Honey's interest in things that indicated she was connected with what was going on. Her disappearance and Joe's arrest. The apparent fear the Lotissivians had for something in the United States. The building of this fantastically gigantic structure. The Lotissivians themselves! Where had they come from? No one knew. They had just appeared and conquered the world in a day, when the world was in the midst of a global war that had lain waste to all Europe as each side rained atom bombs on the troops of the enemy in the battle arena, leaving each other's homeland alone for fear of direct reprisals.

The whole thing swirled round and round in his thoughts, resolving nothing except large blank areas that needed filling in. Thinking couldn't help. Not yet. Instinct, or some sixth sense, whispered to Henry that he was at the focus of forces more immense than the military forces of the Lotissivians— that in some way he held everything in the palm of his hand—that if he could grasp all the threads that dangled around him he could act.

Act in what way? What did he want? What did Major Winthrop want? Permanent occupation by the Lotissivians? Defeat of the alien space horde and a return to the old status quo? What then? What of the strange red devils?

Henry shook his head hopelessly. He was beginning to feel that the major had been right in saying he lacked comprehension and exercised faulty judgement. Even now he might be doing the wrong thing.

The car halted. Henry climbed out, flanked by the M.P.'s. They entered a room where several uniformed men lounged about. An officer sitting behind a desk looked sharply at Henry, then down to a paper on the desk.

"Put him in fourteen. Search him and put all his things in a large envelope."

"Wait a minute," Henry said hastily. "I thought I was being taken to—just why was I picked up? Am I under arrest?"

"You're under arrest," the man behind the desk said.

Henry was reaching into his pocket as he spoke. He casually transferred one of the *charrymns* to his left-hand pocket.

"But why?" he asked. He could feel the strange, exhilarating coolness begin to spread through him.

An M.P. stepped over to him, reaching to take one of his arms. His hand passed through the arm and was buried half way to the elbow.

"What the...?" the man exclaimed.

The room was growing shadowy, unsubstantial. The M.P.'s were shadowy figures running around, even through the same space he stood in. There frantic voices were weak and off tone as they asked each other where he had gone to.

"You are really a man of unsuspected talents, Mr. Prince," a crisp voice sounded at Henry's shoulder.

He turned in the direction of the voice. The being standing there was very similar to the one he had met before, but somewhat larger and redder of skin. And it was very solid in this new world of shadows.

CHAPTER FIVE

"WHO ARE you?" Henry asked. "You aren't the one I saw before."

"No," the being said. "Unfortunately he was captured. It couldn't be helped. Now we must do something, which will probably shock you very much. I'd suggest you close your eyes and trust me completely. It will save you a great deal of mental anguish."

"All right," Henry said, wondering why he did so.

He felt a cool hand grip his wrist. It pulled. He went in the direction it led him.

As unaccountably as he had given into the creature's request he opened his eyes and looked back. He stopped, frozen with horror. In the shadowy world about him he saw a figure lying on the floor, the shadows of the M.P.'s rushing toward it. And the figure on the floor was...his own.

He was only vaguely aware of the next few moments. Later he had a vague memory of jerking away from the grasp of the being and running back to the inert form of shadow, of getting down on his hands and knees and trying to lie in the same position, of feeling something reach out and draw him into that shadowy form.

Then abruptly he was opening his eyes and the shadows were solid again, the M.P.'s quite real and comfortingly solid. He looked around him. The red devil-like creature was gone.

"What happened?" he asked weakly.

The M.P.'s looked at one another doubtfully.

"You fainted—I guess," one of them growled.

Henry stood up shakily. He slipped his right hand into his pocket. It was empty. He looked over at the desk. There was a brown envelope laying there, containing the contents of his pockets.

Right at the moment he didn't care whether the *charrymns* were in that envelope or in the possession of that being.

Another M.P. chuckled nervously.

"We thought for a few minutes you were dead," he said. "You didn't even have a pulse."

"I thought I was dead too," Henry said. He grinned when they looked at him queerly.

"What should we do?" one of them asked the man at the desk. "Take him to Fourteen or the hospital?"

"Fourteen," the man at the desk replied. "We'll get a doctor over later to look at him."

With a strong hand gripping each arm, Henry was led over to a door and through it along a hall. He was stopped before a door numbered fourteen. An M.P. opened the door, stepping to one side. Henry felt himself pushed roughly forward through the doorway. He didn't fall, but before he could stop himself and turn around he heard the door slam, and the sound of the lock being turned with metallic finality.

He looked around, wondering if that red being had followed him. If what he had experienced was any indication, it could be right in the room with him now, seeing him as a shadowy form.

His attention jerked to the wall opposite to where he had entered. There was a second door there, closed. He crossed to it and cautiously twisted the knob, pushing gently. The door opened an inch. He paused before opening it farther.

A light was dawning in his mind. Of course it would have happened this way. He had asked to see Major Winthrop. They didn't want him to come openly, so they had "arrested" him and put him in a cell—which opened into another room where the major was waiting for him.

He pushed the door wide and started to enter. Instantly he was enwrapped in what he numbly recognized as high voltage electric sparks that jumped out from the doorframe and shot into him, jerking his muscles spasmodically.

He leaped forward, aware of the smell of ozone, trying to land on his feet, but falling forward. He landed painfully and lay half dazed, hearing the door he had just come through slam shut.

He lifted himself to his hands and knees and glanced up. Standing in front of him, with a half smile on too-handsome lips in an elfin face dominated by a bulging brow, was the living replica of the many pictures Henry had seen of the Lotissivians.

HENRY turned over and sat on the floor without taking his eyes from the extraterrestrial. There was something just right in the alien proportions of that face and figure. The Lotissivian was about four feet tall and his skin was milky white, his eyes a deep violet bordering on black.

"Nothing seems to have entered with him," a voice said. Henry's eyes jerked in that direction. It belonged to a second Lotissivian. There were several in the room.

"I think I owe you an explanation for this reception," the Lotissivian said, turning back to Henry. "This room is specially constructed for our safety. Its walls are laminated, with alternate layers of metal and insulation, with a difference of potential between each plate high enough to prevent *anything* from passing through. I believe you know what I am referring to?"

Henry nodded.

"The only vulnerable avenue," the Lotissivian went on, "is the doorway. We have done all we can to reduce the risk from that direction to a minimum. The electrical display serves the dual purpose of making it impossible for certain beings to enter by concealing themselves within the space of your body as you enter, and of making them hesitate while you enter until we can get the door closed again and connected to the condenser pattern."

Henry let his eyes explore the room. It was large. At the far end were built-in bunks, enough to accommodate at least fifty people.

"Why am I here?" Henry asked.

"Certain developments have made it necessary," the Lotissivian said. "By the way, my name is Annas. I want you to tell me all you know concerning the disappearance of the girl named Honey Childs."

"But I know absolutely nothing about it," Henry said.

In his thoughts he was trying desperately to make up his mind what to do. Should he trust these Lotissivians? They were the conquerors, and therefore the enemy. They held the Earth in captivity. But he instinctively liked them. He tried to force back the thought that he should trust them completely. It persisted.

"We know you know a great deal about it," Annas said. "Not connected with the direct act of her disappearance, perhaps, but bearing on it."

"I think, I should say nothing," Henry said, "unless allowed to consult with my superior officer and get his instructions."

"Who is your superior officer?" Annas asked.

"If you don't know the answer to that question," Henry said, "then I don't think I should tell you."

"Is it Major Winthrop?"

Henry shrugged without answering. His mind was working at high speed on speculations. He had assumed that his hasty note had been received by the major, and that that was the reason why the M.P.'s had come to get him. When they had put him in a cell under arrest he had doubted. Now, he was doubting again.

Annas spoke in a strange tongue. One of the other Lotissivians went to a desk and lifted a telephone. He dialed a number. After a short wait he spoke into the phone, cupping the mouthpiece so that Henry couldn't hear what was said.

When he hung up he spoke to Annas again in the strange language.

"I see," Annas said. "Major Winthrop says you are one of his undercover agents. We had not known that. You gave yourself away when you asked to speak to your chief. A laborer doesn't have a chief to speak to and get instructions."

He smiled at the stricken expression on Henry's face.

"And for your information," he went on, "Arras did not call Major Winthrop just now. He just pretended to. We have found out what we wanted to know from your reactions. We will now get the major here and discover what is going on."

"Do you know what's happened to Honey Childs?" Henry asked, as the one called Arras went back to the phone.

"No, Mr. Prince," Annas said. "But we are going to find out if we have to tear this entire world into its component atoms. You see, she is a Lotissivian."

"A Lotissivian," Henry gasped. "But—but she doesn't look like you. She's—*human.*"

"And what do you think we are," Annas said coldly. "The Lotissivian female is taller than the male, her brain much smaller, but no less capable I assure you."

"So," Henry breathed. "That accounts for a lot. Poor Joe."

"Yes," Annas said emotionlessly, "he's in love with her. And so are you, which is natural. We have kept secret the fact that Lotissivian females are enough like Earth females of certain types of beauty to pass for natives without any evident trouble."

Henry flushed angrily.

"Maybe I shouldn't say 'Poor Joe' so hastily," he said. "It could be that Honey prefers a man to your type."

He smiled in satisfaction as he saw Annas' face set in harsh lines for a moment.

A MELODIOUS chime sounded one brief note through the room. Annas turned toward the door Henry had come through, an expectant light in his eyes. Henry followed his gaze, saw the knob twist and the door come open.

Major Winthrop stood on the other side. His face was pale, he took a deep breath and jumped forward. There was a flare of electric discharge, then he was through. The door closed again.

"Well, Henry," the major said, "I see you've done it again."

"Yes sir," Henry said, flushing. "I'm not cut out for this work. I know that now. As soon as it's convenient I'll resign."

"Just why did you assume that I had you brought here?" the major asked.

"If I answer that," Henry said angrily, "I will be committing another blunder."

"Well answer it anyway."

"I mailed a request to see you," Henry said. "That was over two hours ago. When the M.P.'s came for me it was a natural assumption that you had sent them."

"I didn't get the note," Major Winthrop said. "Too soon."

"How was I to know it was too soon?" Henry said. "I had assumed that such letters were given speedy delivery."

"This is interesting," Annas cut in. "How are such letters addressed?"

"They're addressed to my department," the major said quickly.

"Aha! You are too quick with the answer," Annas said, delighted. "Tell me how the address reads."

"C.P.O.XXX," Major Winthrop said. "The C.P.O. means 'care of Postmaster,' which takes the letter directly to the postmaster's office where the letter is redirected according to the code letters designating its address. The XXX is the code number for my office."

"But I understood the code letters for your office were U.O.5," Annas said.

"Too many people might know of that," the major said uncomfortably. "To protect Prince we gave our department a special designation for his work."

"Let it go," Annas said, his tone implying that he knew more than they suspected. "Instruct Mr. Prince to tell us all he has accomplished and all he knows relating to the assignment he is on."

"Go ahead, Henry," the major said tonelessly.

"There's a lot I didn't know that I wish now I had," Henry began. "I didn't know Honey Childs was a Lotissivian—"

He saw the sudden look of alarm and self-condemnation appear in Annas' eyes, and the pleased delight in the major's.

"And I didn't know," Henry said slowly, "that the Lotissivians can't touch at least half the population of this planet."

"But the United States isn't half—" the major began, then stopped.

"They could occupy the U. S.," Henry said. "They can conquer every living person on Earth. What they can't do is occupy Hell." He read how close he had hit the mark, in Annas' expression. "Yes," he went on. "There's a lot I don't know even yet. But I can guess. It may be that besides Hell there's the counterpart of what we call Heaven. And until the Lotissivians can invade Heaven and Hell and subdue them, they'll never be complete masters of this planet, or even able to stay here safely. That is, unless this giant building is finished and properly protected all around with high potential condenser barriers to keep out the dead."

"Are you insane?" Major Winthrop said. He studied Annas' expression and shook his head slowly. "No, I guess not. You can't be right, but you must be close to something that is the truth."

"By a remarkable stroke of insight," Annas said. "Mr. Prince has hit upon the truth. But he could not have done so without knowing a great deal that he hasn't told."

"I can't believe it," Major Winthrop said. "That red devil whose corpse we found this morning certainly wasn't a spirit or real devil. He's made of flesh and blood. Solid stuff that the doctor's knife can cut and place under a microscope. Cellular structure that the microscope brings out. The doctor's official opinion in his written report is that the thing is either derived from the human race or a product of convergent evolution of an unrelated type of warm-blooded life. It definitely isn't a soul of a dead person that once lived."

"Sometimes thoughts expressed by you people of Earth are very difficult to grasp," Annas said. "Not because they are deep but because they are couched in incompleteness. However, I gather vaguely what you mean. Do not be surprised if the pieces of this creature your doctor has pasted onto the microscope slides vanish with the rest of him by morning. And now, Major, you will instruct Mr. Prince to tell me everything he knows, and you will leave before he starts talking."

Henry looked keenly at the major, trying to fathom what he should do and hoping the major would give some indication.

"You will tell Annas everything he wishes to know, and co-operate with him in every way, Henry," the major said. But there was the barest suggestion of a twitch to his right eye as he gave the order.

"Yes, sir," Henry said.

"That's all, then," Major Winthrop said, going to the door.

"NOW," ANNAS said when the door had closed. "Now I'm going to do something even your shrewd insight will not have foreseen. I'm not going to ask you anything. I merely wanted the major to think I would. And I didn't miss the wink that countermanded his verbal order."

"Then what are you going to do?" Henry asked, liking this bulging headed midget more and more.

"In spite of your superior officer's low opinion of your judgment, I find it much superior to that of the average Earth being," Annas said. "So I'm going to paint you a word picture. Sit down and relax."

His smile was completely friendly. Henry found himself unable to keep from responding to it as he crossed over to a chair and sat down.

"You may smoke too, if you wish to," Annas said. And, as Henry took out a cigarette and lit it, "You know, it's a real treat to see a man of this planet that I can call my equal in intelligence. And mind you, I'm not trying to flatter you or even impress you. It's a statement of fact. You have divined practically everything, and most of what I want to talk to you about is either known to you or would become immediately apparent if you had the leisure to think it over.

"At present," Annas continued, "you're torn between loyalties and logics. Even your government leaders are the same. In every country we find a strong feeling that it would be better to have continued world anarchy rather than law and order under the light yoke of a race alien to your planet. Emotionally that is your universal reaction. Intellectually you universally recognize that if our domination is impersonal and unselfish, and permits complete liberty to develop life and potentialities so long as they do not inflict trouble on others, then it is much better to submit to us. Actually our coming here is somewhat the same in purpose as your sending missionaries to backward countries. You have nothing we would care to possess or take away with us. Your minerals? We do not need them. Actually, we are gathering and bringing down into Russia from outer space far more of the metals going into this structure than are being mined."

"Where do you come from?" Henry asked. "No one seems to know. From one of the other planets?"

"No. Certainly not," Annas said. "Our force of eight billion is just a small contingent one."

"From the planetary system of some star?" Henry asked.

"Not that either," Annas said. "Originally, of course. But that was long ago. A very long time ago. No, we come from regions in interstellar space where we have constructed thousands of cubic miles of habitable structures similar to this little box-like structure we are having you Earthmen construct here. Most of the races of the Cosmos eventually migrate to interstellar space. Our own, the Lotissivians, are one of the average groups. We number around eighty thousand billion."

"Interstellar space," Henry said. "Why have you bothered with us? I mean, if this invasion of our planet is just a missionary trip to you, why have you made it now rather than in the past?"

"The reason is twofold," Annas said. "First, until you entered the borders of our region your welfare was beyond our jurisdiction. Second, now that you have entered our jurisdiction you are our responsibility. And since you will be here for about four hundred years of your time, we must either get things in order here on your planet in a hurry or have a lot of work ahead of us. We'd like to establish peace and harmony as soon as possible."

"And in four hundred years you will pull up stakes and let the Solar System go its merry way?" Henry asked.

"That's right," Annas said. "And in four hundred years we hope to have brought knowledge to every part of the Earth and raised its living standards so that all countries are as well off as the United States will be by then."

"I'm trying to grasp what you say," Henry said. "It's on too grand a scale for me to take easily. It implies that there is a sort of mapping out of all space like we mark off nations here on the Earth's surface, and that the Solar System is like a train moving across the United States, in which you can drink alcoholic beverages for a couple of hundred miles and then you come to a stretch where it's against the law—because you're in a dry state. What region did we just pass out of before we entered the Lotissivian region of space?"

"Before you entered *Lotissiv? Vetapuissa,*" Annas said calmly.

"And are the Vetapuissans built like you?"

"Very much so," Annas said. "Though probably less so than even you people of Earth."

"Then all intelligent races in the universe had a common origin?"

"No. Definitely not," Annas said. "Your race and mine did not have a common origin. I see you don't believe that. Let me ask you this: Would you believe that sulphur, oxygen, and hydrogen could combine on Mars to form sulphuric acid?"

"Of course," Henry said. "So long as the temperature was such that it could exist."

"All life structures," Annas said, "arise from a basic pattern that is inherent in the properties of matter. It's no more remarkable than sulphuric acid, basically, though almost infinitely more complex."

"I'll have to take your word for that," Henry said. "But answer me this. Suppose there were some scientific principle you haven't yet discovered, and by means of it you Lotissivians were driven away from our planet. What would happen? Are you out to assume full responsibility for our well being, *even if you have to blow us out of existence to do it?*"

"There are no scientific principles we have not discovered," Annas said.

"Thanks," Henry said. "Thanks very much, Annas. You've told me what I wanted to know."

THE ONE named Arras burst out rapidly in his strange language. Annas listened, his face gradually taking on an expression of ludicrous surprise.

As Arras continued, Annas' expression became thoughtful, then bitter, and finally settled into a mold of almost pouting resignation. Arras stopped.

There was a long moment of silence. Annas bowed with great dignity to Henry.

"My respects to one more cunning than I," he said stiffly. "You may leave now, Prince."

Henry's mouth dropped open in astonishment at this sudden development. Annas remained partly bent in a stiff-backed bow, the expression of restrained bitterness on his face.

Henry turned slowly and went to the door, looked back at Annas who remained as he was, unmoving as a statue.

"Look—" Henry began, then stopped, not knowing what to say.

He opened the door and took a deep breath, then jumped through, feeling the electric flames lick at him briefly.

The door closed. He was alone in the small bare room. He tried the outer door. It was unlocked. He pushed it open and went out, and on to the outer office.

The M.P.'s seemed to be expecting him. They returned his things, including the three *charrymns*. He took them, hiding his bewilderment and amazement.

"We'll take you back to your quarters," one of them said, smiling politely, though he detected something close to fear lurking in the man's eyes.

"Okay," he said, taking each object from the envelope and dropping it in his pockets.

He waited until the last with the three *charrymns*, leaving them in plain sight on the desktop. Henry looked at him sharply and the one belonging to Al was still tightly wrapped in the napkin. He placed it and one of the other two in his right hand pocket. Last, he picked up the third one, holding it in his hand.

The now familiar soothing coolness was creeping from the *charrymn* in his hand up into his arm.

The memory of the nightmare he had experienced a short hour before struck him with all its horror. Instantly he dropped the *charrymn* into his pocket with the other two.

But just before it left his hand he had a fleeting impression of seeing that red creature step past him as though coming from behind. Then the three *charrymns* were nestled together in his pocket, and everything seemed normal.

He looked around, smiling. The face of every man in the room was deadly white.

"What's the matter with you guys?" Henry asked. "Seen a ghost?"

"Come on, Pri—" The man who spoke turned abruptly and started toward the exit.

The four M.P's were silent as they drove back to the dorm building. When Henry climbed out they sped away, not looking back.

Feeling that the whole world was more than slightly askew, Henry went into the building. The overhead lights were out, leaving only the small wall lights to cast a faint illumination.

He walked softly down the aisles between rows of cots until he came to his own. He stopped abruptly, surprised. Joe was in his own bed, sound asleep. Joe was back.

He undressed, slid into his blankets, closed his eyes, then opened them again because the red haze that rose in his mind was worse than the semidarkness. But they wouldn't stay open. Finally he gave in and left them closed, while the red haze grew deeper and deeper in color and depth. There seemed to be movement in it, vague movements as though unseen things were moving about, disturbing it by setting up currents.

"Just the blood in my eyelids," he muttered wearily.

ALMOST IN answer, something white appeared at the border of his vision. There seemed to be shape to it, an elusive shape that seemed to come toward him. Something heavy came to rest against his shoulder. Its weight was comforting, soothing. The tiredness in his body seemed to retreat from the weight on his shoulder.

The white shape was becoming clearer now. It had a face. Joe's face.

"This is remarkable," he thought. "I can see Joe bending over me, and my eyes are closed."

He could see the face quite clearly now. It was Joe, but a different Joe than he had seen in waking life. The features were unmistakably the same, but in some indefinable way they seemed to embody what he had sensed in the Lotissivians. A rightness. Perfection.

Perfection! A surge of intense hatred flooded through him. An impulse took hold of him to rise up and strike at Joe. It died as quickly as it appeared, leaving him weak. He marveled at it. He had never before experienced such intense hatred. It was a completely new emotional experience. It was like all the other things he had been experiencing. Insane things.

Like the things he had said when he was with Annas. He didn't know what he said, really. He had just said things. And Annas had been very impressed. That was odd, too.

As when he had put on a knowing look after Annas had said that the Lotissivians knew every scientific principle, and he had said, "Thanks. Thanks very much. That's what I wanted to know." Crazy. But not half as crazy as Annas' and Arras' reaction.

Egotistical little shrimps, the Lotissivians, thinking they knew everything, when they didn't know about the *charrymns* and how, by placing them on either side of you, you could slip over a little ways into the plane or place of state, or whatever it was, where the red devils were.

Egotistical. No wonder they hadn't asked him any questions. They thought they knew everything.

But suppose they did? Suppose they knew all about the *charrymns* too? Something clicked in Henry's mind, and he knew suddenly that Annas did know about the *charrymns*.

But if he knew, then why didn't the Lotissivians use that knowledge to build weapons that could enable them to conquer Hell itself?

It was crazy. And that devil lying in the street, dead. How could a devil die? It must be that even the dead can die. But these devils weren't dead. They were alive, only in a different kind of existence, like when he himself lay dead and was still alive in that other place, and went back and lay down and crawled back into his body and it came to life again.

There was something there, if he could only pin it down. It wasn't superstition or religion, but something real. Something that was a part of nature, just as intelligent races always have human shape became that is the inevitable nature of the evolvement of life from inert matter. Just as sulphuric acid made on Mars wouldn't be evolved from sulphuric acid made on Earth, though it would be the same stuff.

It was inevitable. Everything was inevitable. If he could see things clearly as they really were he would know what to do. That was what Annas was trying to do, make him see everything as it really was. And that was what Major Winthrop had tried to do. The major had said his judgment was faulty because he didn't have a proper grasp of things. Annas had said his judgment was better than any other person's. Flattery. But they had both been right. That was funny, too. They said opposite things and were both right.

He looked up into the white, infinitely kind face hovering over him. Joe's face and yet not Joe's face. He was looking up at it, and yet his eyes were closed tight.

He began to shudder. The pressure, the comforting pressure of Joe's hand on his shoulder, increased. The shuddering became sobbing. He knew he wasn't making any noise, but he was crying. He hadn't cried since he was a baby. Then why was he crying?

He hung onto that question in his thoughts, revolving it around. It was tied in with all the other things that had happened. It was as though his whole emotional complex had gone haywire.

Suddenly, in one convulsive move, he sat up and opened his eyes, feeling Joe's hand slide from his shoulder as he did so. The answer had come to him in that instant.

"Everyone there knew it except me," he said softly.

"Knew what?" Joe growled.

"That I was *the* Prince," Henry answered.

"AL," JOE hissed. "Wake up, Al."

"Huh?" Al's voice sounded. He sat up, blinking. "Oh, you're back."

"We've got to get dressed and take Hank to the doctor," Joe whispered.

"I don't need to go to the doctor," Henry said, his teeth chattering.

"You need something to quiet your nerves," Joe said. "Come on, Al, wake up."

"I'm awake," Al said. He slid to the foot of his cot and started getting dressed.

"Take care of Hank while I get some clothes on," Joe said.

"But I don't want to see the doctor," Henry said insistently.

He struggled to free himself from Joe's grasp.

"Hold him, Al. Don't let him get away," Joe said. He dressed quickly. "Now we'll get him dressed," he said.

He picked up Henry's trousers.

"Stick out your legs, Hank," he ordered quietly.

"No," Henry said.

"Come on, Hank," Al murmured.

Henry struggled more violently. Al had his arms pinned behind him. He looked meaningfully at Joe.

Joe nodded sadly, leaned forward, and tapped Henry just under the ear.

"Neat," Al said as Henry went slack. "What happened to him?"

"I don't know," Joe muttered, slipping Henry's trousers on him. "I think this business is too big for us. I wish we were out of it."

"What's the matter?" someone asked from another cot.

"Hank's sick," Joe said. "We're taking him to the doctor."

Supporting Henry between them they made their way along the aisles.

"Keep an eye on him while I drop a note to the major," Joe said.

They eased him into a chair. Joe looked down at Henry's relaxed features, his eyes full of pity. Then he went into the reading room and wrote hastily, covering both sides of the paper. Then he sealed the letter and dropped it into the mailbox.

When he returned he was just in time to see Al strike something out of Henry's hand.

Henry leaped from the chair and dived after the rolling object. It came toward Joe who reached down and caught it, holding it up to look at it. When he saw what it was he dropped it quickly into his pocket and looked around uneasily. It had been one of the *charrymns*.

"Give me that," Henry said.

"Don't do it, Joe," Al warned. "He was trying to call up that red devil."

"No I wasn't," Henry said. "I was trying to do something else. I have two more of them, you know. But it takes all three to do what I was going to do."

"Tell us about it, Hank," Joe said.

"It's something I discovered," Henry said eagerly. "With two of them in my pocket and the third one in my hand or the other pocket, I can slip over to where they come from. Give it back to me and I'll show you."

"Suppose you give me the two you have and let me try it myself," Joe said.

"No," Henry said. "It was my idea."

He held out his hand imperiously, his eyes feverish. Joe saw Al stealing up behind Henry. He reached toward his pocket slowly, giving Al time to reach him.

Al shoved Henry forward. Joe hit him on the chin, then caught him as he slumped toward the floor.

"Absolutely crazy," Al murmured.

"No, I don't think so," Joe said. "Let's get him to the doctor. But first—" He reached into Henry's pocket and brought out the other two charrymns, dropping them into his pocket with the other one. "Now he can't try anything with these things."

"HOLD HIM, boys," the doctor said. "I've got to have him still or I can't get the needle in."

"You're crazy to do this, Joe," Henry shouted. "Crazy, do you hear? You've been tricked. She isn't human. She's a Lotissivian. Let her rot in hell. You can't go there. They'll kill her if you try it."

"Okay," the doctor said, pulling out the empty needle.

Joe and Al hung on grimly as Henry's struggling weakened, the light of madness dying out in his eyes. When his movements ceased they released him and stepped back.

"He'll be all right now, boys," the doctor said. "That'll last him all night. In the morning before he wakes up we'll put a straitjacket on him. Know him long?"

"Yeah," Joe said. "A long time. Come on, Al. Let's go."

The floor under his feet shook slightly. A rumbling, almost inaudible roar seemed to emanate from the walls.

"Quick," Joe said. He ran to the door and out of the hospital building, Al following him.

The quake was not repeated, but the atmosphere was heavy and thick. An electric tension seemed to be everywhere. In the distance things seemed to merge into a reddish haze.

A strange crackling sound began. It grew until it sounded like the rustling of millions of ants marching to battle. The metal they ran across became luminous. Electric flame of deep violet licked upward from it, forming a carpet of radiant violet fire. It was spreading, driving into the red haze, dissipating it.

"There's a truck over there," Joe shouted.

He ran to it. Al climbed in as he started the motor. In a moment the truck was speeding through the blue fire and red fog toward the distant wall of the upper level.

A bolt of lightning zagged down from above, crashing into the floor across which they raced. It left a smoking, glowing hole. Joe spun the wheel, narrowly missing the gap.

Another bolt struck to the right of the truck. Then another and another.

"The fools," Joe muttered. He hugged the wheel closer, his eyes wary.

Al clung to his seat, staring alternately at Joe and the holocaust outside. Joe, sensing his stare flashed him a grin.

"We'll make it," he said.

"What makes you so sure?" Al grunted.

"I don't know," Joe said, frowning, his eyes intent on the roadway ahead.

A flash of lightning came toward them. It broke and spread out in an umbrella shape that fell completely around the speeding truck.

"See what I mean?" Joe said. "That would have been a direct hit. What stopped it like that? I don't know, but I felt that nothing could touch us. Nothing can touch us. I don't know why, but I know it's so."

They reached the tunnel that led into the upper structure. With unabated speed Joe drove along it. He went deeper and deeper. At last he braked to an abrupt stop. He was out of the truck and running into a small corridor by the time Al had opened the door on his side.

"Hurry, Al," he called back.

The floor underfoot was shaking again, more violently than before. A rumbling roar rose to deafening proportions. They reached a door and pulled it open.

Inside, several men in military police uniforms jumped up in surprise and started forward. Then they fell back, their faces paling perceptibly. They were ignoring Al, staring at Joe.

Suddenly Al, too, stopped in his tracks, staring. For something was happening to Joe.

He seemed to be enveloped in an aura of white radiance. And he had stopped running now.

He stood in the center of the room, an air of expectancy on his face. Al saw him reach into a pocket and bring something out in his fist.

Then slowly he faded from sight.

CHAPTER SIX

"I TELL YOU *I don't know* what happened then," Joe said. "I held one of the three *charrymns* in my hand like Hank had said he did. I saw everybody staring at me like they were seeing a ghost. You did too, Al." He grinned at Al. "The room and everyone in it faded until everything I had been looking at before was shadowy. Like fog with definite shape to it. But other things were coming into sight. Remember that red fog, Al? It *really* got red. It glowed red like fire in a furnace. But around me everything was free of the red light. A wisp would dart in and dissolve into nothing before it could reach me. And in that red, glowing fog were dozens of those fellows with pointed ears. I just got a brief impression of them, and of one that seemed to literally radiate force.

"Then suddenly I seemed to be caught up in a storm of white light. I felt— There aren't words even to begin to describe how I felt. Like a god. I was a god. I was a huge sun radiating heat that withered everything around me, yet I was cool. I was a harmless old man radiating kindness. I was—oh what's the use. It was like standing in the middle of a factory and trying to imagine yourself as *being* the factory. Actually I was the center of something going on around me, focused through me, like light is focused through a lens. I seemed to know everything and understand everything, and now I can't even remember much of it. I knew that those three *charrymns* were what made the whole thing possible. You held the key, Hank, and didn't know it. It was those *charrymns*, the way they worked when one human being had them."

"But the Lotissivians knew about them," Henry said.

"Not what you knew about them," Joe said. "Your namesake, the Prince, put that thought in your head to keep it a secret. We were both puppets. That's all. Puppets."

"What about me?" Honey Childs asked.

"You were a goat staked out for the lion."

"Are you sure you aren't a Lotissivian, Honey?" Henry asked. "Annas said you were."

"The reason he said she was," Joe said, "was because he wasn't talking to you then. He was talking to your namesake."

"No," Honey said. A queer, cramped expression crossed her face. "I was a Lotissivian. Just like you were Satan, Hank, and you were God, Joe. Only I was a Lotissivian for days and days, while you two were what you were for just moments. The Lotissivians know all about it. I learned something about it while she and I were together.

"Atoms act on one another like keys and locks act on one another. Or like radio broadcasters and receivers act together. When I was the Lotissivian woman I was still there, but sort of outside my body. And she was inside."

"Like when I saw myself lying on the floor and crawled back into myself," Henry said.

"That's it," Honey said. "That's it exactly. The Lotissivian girl said I couldn't know what really went on because all I could see or sense was what the ideas in my mind fitted. All the rest passed over my head like it wasn't there. And half of what I thought I saw or experienced wasn't true, but only symbolic of what happened, like dreams are symbolic of things going on in the subconscious that the censor of the mind won't let come into consciousness." She shuddered suddenly. "I was just remembering that awful ride back up on that beam that was being lifted from the ground."

THE DOOR opened. Major Winthrop came in.

"Trying to figure things out?" he asked. "I'd suggest you don't try. Your plane will be ready to take off as soon as you get on board."

He sat down in an empty chair.

"I think you understand the reason you have to go back to the States. All of you," he said. "You're no good to us any more. You've been through too much and you're too vulnerable now to the forces still loose in the world, the forces we used to call the forces of darkness. I want you to try to look at things my way. It'll be easier for you to forget.

"Consider some little tribe of savages that for generations has never been a hundred miles from where it was born. One day a mechanized army shows up, then another, and there's a big battle. After that prefabricated houses are put up, refrigerators make ice cubes, radios blare music, helicopters drop out of the sky and bring other people and take some that were there.

"The natives try to understand how the radio picks music out of the air around them, how the refrigerator takes the water dipped out of the river and turns it to ice that can melt and be river water again. They try to understand that the evil spirit that comes from the god in the volcano to punish them is nothing but germs that can be seen through a microscope.

"Get the idea? We're just like that. From the cosmic point of view we're just a little ball of matter with a couple of billion planet-imprisoned people on it. We've denied the existence of a lot of things we didn't know how to explain, or we've been superstitious about them. We're faced now with the realization that we're still savages ignorant of most of the basic things, unable to adjust our minds to the things the Lotissivians consider commonplace.

"Things are pretty much straightened out now. With the help of a big and powerful tribal chieftain on the other side of the mountain, so to speak, a tribe of cannibals has been wiped out.

"And there's great promise that our grandchildren will have a chance to learn how ice cubes come from river water.

"What you went through was no more incomprehensible in its way than the native using the white man's firestick to blow the head off an enemy while fainting at the recoil against his shoulder and the big noise it makes. Everything's relative.

"Take this gigantic building the Lotissivians are going to leave their permanent occupation force in. It's on no grander a scale for them than it would be for the missionary to have the natives make mud bricks and build him a three-story house.

"The analogy makes everything fairly understandable. Even that red devil that got killed when you were being kidnapped after you dropped Joe off that night, Honey. Remember, Henry, that Annas said he'd vanish, and even the sections of him on the microscope slides would disappear?" Major Winthrop grinned and spread his arms. "The *ice cube* melted as he said it would."

"That was terrible—and strange," Honey said. "Those strange creatures were materializing out of thin air, and all of a sudden I seemed to have the power to glow all over. Then that one ran into me and dropped to the ground. After that—"

A look of terror crossed her face. She started to tremble.

"Forget about it," Major Winthrop said. "Most of the horror of it rises from fear of the unknown. The same thing that scares the wits out of you if something taps you on the shoulder when you walk through a cemetery alone at night."

HIS CONFIDENT chuckle was infectious. Honey stopped trembling.

"I wish you'd come with us, Major," she said. "You make it all seem so—ordinary. When I stood on that big beam being raised up from the supply platform and I started to get solid again that man nearly jumped off, he was so frightened."

"Where were you before you got on that beam?" Al asked.

"I—oh, don't ask me. I don't know. I don't know!" Honey started to cry.

"Why don't you keep your mouth shut?" Joe growled. "She was in Hell. Do you expect her to remember that?"

"Not Hell," Major Winthrop said. "That's just a myth, like the angry god in the volcano. Say she was in the hands of a tribe of cannibals. Human beings, but a different tribe in a different land, more bestial, maybe incurably barbaric."

The major stood up and went to the door.

"Time for you to go," he said. "Try to find happiness in your grass huts back home. And whenever you remember and get afraid, try to think of the native in Africa who met an ice cube for the first time."

He stood in the doorway watching as they crossed to the plane. They turned and waved at him, then disappeared inside. Shortly the plane moved across the flat metal expanse and took to the air.

He shaded his eyes to watch it until it vanished in the distance, then looked up at the silver flashes signaling the presence of the Lotissivian spaceships circling the Earth inside the Moon's orbit as the sunlight struck them and reflected downward.

"Did I do all right, Annas?" he whispered. And several miles away in the protected chamber the too-beautiful lips of the Lotissivian broke into a kindly smile.

"Right, indeed, Major," he murmured.

THE END

If you've enjoyed this book, you will not want to miss these terrific titles...

ARMCHAIR SCI-FI & HORROR DOUBLE NOVELS, $12.95 each

D-71 **THE DEEP END** by Gregory Luce
TO WATCH BY NIGHT by Robert Moore Williams

D-72 **SWORDSMAN OF LOST TERRA** by Poul Anderson
PLANET OF GHOSTS by David V. Reed

D-73 **MOON OF BATTLE** by J. J. Allerton
THE MUTANT WEAPON by Murray Leinster

D-74 **OLD SPACEMEN NEVER DIE!** John Jakes
RETURN TO EARTH by Bryan Berry

D-75 **THE THING FROM UNDERNEATH** by Milton Lesser
OPERATION INTERSTELLAR by George O. Smith

D-76 **THE BURNING WORLD** by Algis Budrys
FOREVER IS TOO LONG by Chester S. Geier

D-77 **THE COSMIC JUNKMAN** by Rog Phillips
THE ULTIMATE WEAPON by John W. Campbell

D-78 **THE TIES OF EARTH** by James H. Schmitz
CUE FOR QUIET by Thomas L. Sherred

D-79 **SECRET OF THE MARTIANS** by Paul W. Fairman
THE VARIABLE MAN by Philip K. Dick

D-80 **THE GREEN GIRL** by Jack Williamson
THE ROBOT PERIL by Don Wilcox

ARMCHAIR SCIENCE FICTION CLASSICS, $12.95 each

C-25 **THE STAR KINGS**
by Edmond Hamilton

C-26 **NOT IN SOLITUDE**
by Kenneth Gantz

C-32 **PROMETHEUS II**
by S. J. Byrne

ARMCHAIR SCI-FI & HORROR GEMS SERIES, $12.95 each

G-7 **SCIENCE FICTION GEMS, Vol. Four**
Jack Sharkey and others

G-8 **HORROR GEMS, Vol. Four**
Seabury Quinn and others

If you've enjoyed this book, you will not want to miss these terrific titles…

ARMCHAIR SCI-FI & HORROR DOUBLE NOVELS, $12.95 each

D-81   **THE LAST PLEA** by Robert Bloch
        THE STATUS CIVILIZATION by Robert Sheckley

D-82   **WOMAN FROM ANOTHER PLANET** by Frank Belknap Long
        HOMECALLING by Judith Merril

D-83   **WHEN TWO WORLDS MEET** by Robert Moore Williams
        THE MAN WHO HAD NO BRAINS by Jeff Sutton

D-84   **THE SPECTRE OF SUICIDE SWAMP** by E. K. Jarvis
        IT'S MAGIC, YOU DOPE! by Jack Sharkey

D-85   **THE STARSHIP FROM SIRIUS** by Rog Phillips
        FINAL WEAPON by Everett Cole

D-86   **TREASURE ON THUNDER MOON** by Edmond Hamilton
        TRAIL OF THE ASTROGAR by Henry Haase

D-87   **THE VENUS ENIGMA** by Joe Gibson
        THE WOMAN IN SKIN 13 by Paul W. Fairman

D-88   **THE MAD ROBOT** by William P. McGivern
        THE RUNNING MAN by J. Holly Hunter

D-89   **VENGEANCE OF KYVOR** by Randall Garrett
        AT THE EARTH'S CORE by Edgar Rice Burroughs

D-90   **DWELLERS OF THE DEEP** by Don Wilcox
        NIGHT OF THE LONG KNIVES by Fritz Leiber

ARMCHAIR SCIENCE FICTION CLASSICS, $12.95 each

C-28   **THE MAN FROM TOMORROW**
        by Stanton A. Coblentz

C-29   **THE GREEN MAN OF GRAYPEC**
        by Festus Pragnell

C-30   **THE SHAVER MYSTERY, Book Four**
        by Richard S. Shaver

ARMCHAIR MASTERS OF SCIENCE FICTION SERIES, $16.95 each

MS-7   **MASTERS OF SCIENCE FICTION AND FANTASY, Vol. Seven**
        Lester del Rey, "The Band Played On" and other tales

MS-8   **MASTERS OF SCIENCE FICTION, Vol. Eight**
        Milton Lesser, "'A' as in Android" and other tales

If you've enjoyed this book, you will not want to miss these terrific titles…

ARMCHAIR SCI-FI & HORROR DOUBLE NOVELS, $12.95 each

D-91   **THE TIME TRAP** by Henry Kuttner
THE LUNAR LICHEN by Hal Clement

D-92   **SARGASSO OF LOST STARSHIPS** by Poul Anderson
THE ICE QUEEN by Don Wilcox

D-93   **THE PRINCE OF SPACE** by Jack Williamson
POWER by Harl Vincent

D-94   **PLANET OF NO RETURN** by Howard Browne
THE ANNIHILATOR COMES by Ed Earl Repp

D-95   **THE SINISTER INVASION** by Edmond Hamilton
OPERATION TERROR by Murray Leinster

D-96   **TRANSIENT** by Ward Moore
THE WORLD-MOVER by George O. Smith

D-97   **FORTY DAYS HAS SEPTEMBER** by Milton Lesser
THE DEVIL'S PLANET by David Wright O'Brien

D-98   **THE CYBERENE** by Rog Phillips
BADGE OF INFAMY by Lester del Rey

D-99   **THE JUSTICE OF MARTIN BRAND** by Raymond A. Palmer
BRING BACK MY BRAIN by Dwight V. Swain

D-100   **WIDE-OPEN PLANET** by L. Sprague de Camp
AND THEN THE TOWN TOOK OFF by Richard Wilson

ARMCHAIR SCIENCE FICTION CLASSICS, $12.95 each

C-31   **THE GOLDEN GUARDSMEN**
by S. J. Byrne

C-32   **ONE AGAINST THE MOON**
by Donald A. Wollheim

C-33   **HIDDEN CITY**
by Chester S. Geier

ARMCHAIR SCI-FI & HORROR GEMS SERIES, $12.95 each

G-9   **SCIENCE FICTION GEMS, Vol. Five**
Clifford D. Simak and others

G-10   **HORROR GEMS, Vol. Five**
E. Hoffman Price and others

If you've enjoyed this book, you will not want to miss these terrific titles...

ARMCHAIR SCI-FI & HORROR DOUBLE NOVELS, $12.95 each

D-101 **THE CONQUEST OF THE PLANETS** by John W. Campbell
THE MAN WHO ANNEXED THE MOON by Bob Olsen

D-102 **WEAPON FROM THE STARS** by Rog Phillips
THE EARTH WAR by Mack Reynolds

D-103 **THE ALIEN INTELLIGENCE** by Jack Williamson
INTO THE FOURTH DIMENSION by Ray Cummings

D-104 **THE CRYSTAL PLANETOIDS** by Stanton A. Coblentz
SURVIVORS FROM 9,000 B. C. by Robert Moore Williams

D-105 **THE TIME PROJECTOR** by David H. Keller, M.D. and David Lasser
STRANGE COMPULSION by Philip Jose Farmer

D-106 **WHOM THE GODS WOULD SLAY** by Paul W. Fairman
MEN IN THE WALLS by William Tenn

D-107 **LOCKED WORLDS** by Edmond Hamilton
THE LAND THAT TIME FORGOT by Edgar Rice Burroughs

D-108 **STAY OUT OF SPACE** by Dwight V. Swain
REBELS OF THE RED PLANET by Charles L. Fontenay

D-109 **THE METAMORPHS** by S. J. Byrne
MICROCOSMIC BUCCANEERS by Harl Vincent

D-110 **YOU CAN'T ESCAPE FROM MARS** by E. K. Jarvis
THE MAN WITH FIVE LIVES by David V. Reed

ARMCHAIR SCIENCE FICTION CLASSICS, $12.95 each

C-34 **30 DAY WONDER**
by Richard Wilson

C-35 **G.O.G. 666**
by John Taine

C-36 **RALPH 124C 41+**
by Hugo Gernsback

ARMCHAIR SCI-FI & HORROR GEMS SERIES, $12.95 each

G-11 **SCIENCE FICTION GEMS, Vol. Six**
Edmond Hamilton and others

G-12 **HORROR GEMS, Vol. Six**
H. P. Lovecraft and others

IN THE DAYS OF THE TWENTY-FIRST CENTURY...

...war had completely changed. Most large conventional weapons—with the exception of machine guns—were a thing of the past. Even atomic weapons were no longer used. The weapon of choice—gliders! You see, to keep the peace in this strange world of the future, the forces of both the East and West had agreed to disallow all weapons that had been developed before 1900. And war was limited to disputes between unions and corporations. It seemed to be an effective way of keeping the world from destroying itself. But then an ambitious military officer decided to move beyond the prescribed limitations—and soon the world was in deadly peril again.

Join sci-fi great Mack Reynolds as he delivers a fast-moving tale of intrigue and future combat!

To my loyal fans.
Major Joe Maddeer

THE EARTH WAR

WAR

By
MACK REYNOLDS

ARMCHAIR FICTION
PO Box 4369, Medford, Oregon   97501-0168

For more information about Armchair Books and products, visit our website at…

www.armchairfiction.com

Or email us at…

armchairfiction@yahoo.com

CHAPTER ONE

In other eras he might have been described as swacked, stewed, stoned, smashed, crocked, cockeyed, soused, shellacked, polluted, potted, tanked, lit, stinko, pie-eyed, three sheets in the wind, or simply drunk.

In his own time, Major Joseph Mauser, Category Military, Mid-Middle Caste, was drenched.

Or at least rapidly getting there.

He wasn't happy about it. It wasn't that kind of a binge.

He lowered one eyelid and concentrated on the list of potables offered by the auto-bar. He'd decided earlier in the game that it would be a physical impossibility to get through the whole list but he was making a strong attempt on a representative of each subdivision. He'd had a cocktail, a highball, a sour, a flip, a punch and a julep. He wagged forth a finger to dial a fizz, a Sloe Gin Fizz.

Joe Mauser occupied a small table in a corner of the Middle Caste Category Military Club in Greater Washington. His current fame, transient though it might be, would have made him welcome as a guest in the Upper Caste Club, located in the swank Baltimore section of town. Old pros in the Category Military had comparatively small sufferance for caste lines among themselves; rarified class distinctions meant little when you were in the dill, and you didn't become an old pro without having been in spots where matters had pickled. Joe would have been welcome on the strength of his performance in the most recent fracas in which he had participated as a mercenary, that between Vacuum Tube

Transport and Continental Hovercraft. But he didn't want it that way.

You didn't devote the greater part of your life to pulling your way up, pushing your way up, fighting your way up, the ladder of status to be satisfied to associate with your social superiors on the basis of being a nine-day-wonder, an oddity to be met at cocktail parties and spoken to for a few democratic moments.

No, Joe Mauser would stick to his own position in the scheme of things until through his own efforts he won through to that rarefied altitude in society which his ambition demanded.

A sour voice said, "Celebrating, captain? Oops, major, I mean. So you did get something out of the Catskill Reservation fracas. I'm surprised."

A scowl, Joe decided, would be the best. Various others, in the course of the evening, had attempted to join him. Three or four comrades in arms, one journalist from some fracas buff magazine, some woman he'd never met before, and Zen knew how she'd ever got herself into the club. A snarl had driven some away, or a growl or sneer. This one, he decided, called for an angered scowl, particularly in view of the tone of voice which only brought home doubly how his planning of a full two years had come a cropper.

He looked up, beginning his grimace of discouragement. "Go away," he muttered nastily. The other's identity came through slowly. One of the Telly news reporters who'd covered the fracas; for the moment he couldn't recall the name.

Joe Mauser held the common prejudices of the Category Military for Telly and all its ramifications. Not only for the drooling multitudes who sat before their sets and vicariously participated in the sadism of combat while their trank bemused brains refused contemplation of the reality of their way of life. But also for Category Communications, and particularly its Sub-division Telly, Branch Fracas News, and all connected with it. His views, perhaps, were akin to those of the matador facing the moment of truth, the crowds screaming in the arena seats for him to go in and the promoters and managers watching from the *barrera* and possibly wondering if he were gored if next week's gate would improve.

The Telly cameras which watched you as, crouched almost double, you scurried into the fire area of a mitrailleuse or perhaps a Maxim; the Telly cameras which swung in your direction speedily, avidly, when a blast of fire threw you back and to the ground; the Telly cameras with their zoom lenses which focused full into your face as life leaked away. The Spanish aficionados never had it so good. The close-up expression of the dying matador had been denied them.

The other undeterred, sank into the chair opposite, his face twisted cynically. Joe placed him now. Freddy Soligen. Give the man his due, he and his team were right in there when the going got hot. More than once, in the past fifteen years, Joe had seen the little man lugging his cameras into the center of the fracas, taking chances expected only of combatants. Vaguely, he wondered why.

He demanded, "Why?"

"Eh?" Soligen said. "Major, by the looks of you, you're going to have a beaut, comes morning. Why don't you stick to trank?"

"Cause I'm not a slob," Joe sneered. "Why?"

"Why, what? Listen, you want me to help you on home?"

"Got no home. Live in hotels. Military clubs. In barracks. Got nothing but my rank and caste." He sneered again. "Such as they are."

Soligen said, "Mid-Middle, aren't you? And a major. Zen, most would say you haven't much to complain about."

Joe grunted contempt, but dropped that angle of it. However, he could have mentioned that he was well into his thirties, that he had copped many a one in his day and that now time was borrowed. When you had been in the dill as often as had Joe Mauser, the days you lived were borrowed. Borrowed from some lad who hadn't used up all that nature had originally allotted him. He was well into the thirties and his life's goal was still tantalizingly far before him, and he living on borrowed time.

He said, "Why're you...exception? How come you get right into the middle of it, like that time on the Panhandle Reservation. You coulda copped one there."

Soligen chuckled abruptly, and as though in self-deprecation. "I *did* cop one there. Hospitalized three months. Didn't read any of the publicity I got? No, I guess you didn't, it was mostly in the Category Communications trade press. Anyway, I got bounced not only in rank on the job, but up to Low-Middle in caste." There was the faintest edge of the surly in his voice as he added, "I was born a Lower, major."

Joe snorted. "So was I. You didn't answer my question, Soligen. Why stick your neck out? Most of you Telly reporters, stick it out in some concrete pillbox with lots of telescopic equipment." He added bitterly, "And usually away from what's really going on."

The Telly reporter looked at him oddly. "Stick my neck out?" he said with deliberation. "Possibly for the same reason you do, major. In fact, it's kinda the reason I looked you up. Trouble is, you're probably too drenched, right now, to listen to my fling."

Joe Mauser's voice attempted cold dignity. He said, "In the Category Military, Soligen, you never get so drenched you can't operate."

The other's cynical grunt conveyed nothing, but he reached out and dialed the auto-bar. He growled, "O.K., a Sober-Up for you, an ale for me."

"I don't want to sober up. I'm being bitter and enjoying it."

"Yes, you do," the little man said. "I have the answer to your bitterness." He handed Joe the pill. "You see, what's wrong with you, major, is you've been trying to do it alone. What you need is help."

Joe glowered at him, even as he accepted the medication. "I make my own way, Soligen. I don't even know what you're talking about."

"That's obvious," the other said sourly. He waited, sipping his brew, while the Sober-Up worked its miracle. He was compassionate enough to shudder, having been through, in his time, the speeding up of a hangover so that full agony was compressed into mere minutes rather than dispensed over a period of hours.

Joe groaned, "It better be good, whatever you want to say."

Freddy Soligen asked, at long last, tilting his head to one side and taking Joe in critically. "You know one of the big reasons you're only a major?"

Joe Mauser looked at him.

The Telly reporter said, "You haven't got any mustache."

Joe Mauser stared at him.

The other laughed cynically. "You think I'm drivel-happy, eh? Well, maybe a long scar down the cheek would do even better. Or, possibly, you ought to wear a monocle, even in action."

Joe continued to stare, as though the little man had gone completely around the bend.

Freddy Soligen had made his first impression. He finished the ale, put the glass into the chute and turned back to the professional mercenary. His voice was flat now, all expression gone from his face. "All right," he said. "Now listen to my fling. You've got a lot to learn."

Joe held his peace, if only in pure amazement. He ranked the little man opposite him in both caste and in professional attainments. Besides which, he was a combat officer and unused to being addressed with less than full respect, even from superiors. For unlucky Joe Mauser might be in his chosen field, but respected he was.

Freddy Soligen pointed a finger at him, almost mockingly. "You're on the make, Mauser. In a world where few bother, any more, you're on the way up. The trouble is, you took the wrong path many years ago."

Joe snorted his contempt of the other's lack of knowledge. "I was born into the Clothing Category, Sub-division Shoes, Branch Repair. In the old days they called us cobblers. You think you could work your way up from Mid-Lower to Upper caste with that beginning, Soligen? Zen! we don't even have cobblers any more, shoes are thrown away as soon as they show wear. Sure, sure, sure. Theoretically, under People's Capitalism, you can cross categories into any field you want. But have you ever heard of anybody doing any real jumping of caste levels in any category except Military or Religion? I didn't take the wrong path, religion is a little too strong for even my stomach, which left the Category Military the only path available."

Freddy had heard him out, his face twisted sourly. He said now, "You misunderstand. I realize that the military's the only quick way of getting a bounce in caste. I wish I'd figured that out sooner, before I made a trade out of the one I was born into, Communications. It's too late now, I'm into my forties with a busted marriage but the proud papa of a kid." He twisted his face again in another grimace. "By the way, the boy's a novitiate in Category Religion."

Some elements were clearing up in Joe's mind. He said, in comprehension, "So...we're both ambitious."

"That's right, major. Now, let's get back to fundamentals. Your wrong path is the *manner* in which you're trying to work your way up into the elite. You've got to become a celebrated hero, major. And it's the Telly fan, the fracas-buff, who decides who the Category Military heroes are. Those are the slobs you have to toady to. In the long run, nobody else counts. I know, I know. All the old pros, even big names like Stonewall Cogswell and Jack Alshuler, think you're a top man. Great! But how many buff-clubs you got to your name? How often do the buff magazines run articles about you? How often do you get interviewed on Telly, in between fracases? Have the movies ever done 'The Joe Mauser Story'?"

Joe twisted uncomfortably. "All that stuff takes a lot of time. I've been keeping myself busy."

"Right. Busy getting shot at."

"I'm a mercenary. That's my trade."

Freddy spread his hands. "O.K. If that's all you're interested in, shooting lads signed up on the other side, or getting shot by them, that's fine. But you know, major..." He cocked his head to one side, and peered knowingly at Joe. "...I've got a sneaking suspicion that you don't particularly like combat. Some do, I know. Some love it. I don't think you do."

Joe looked at him.

Freddy said, "You're in it because of the chance for promotion, nothing else counts."

Joe remained silent.

Freddy pushed him. "Who're the names every fracas buff knows? Jerry Sturgeon, captain at the age of twenty-one, and so damned pretty in those fancy uniforms he wears. How many times have you ever heard of him really being in the dill? He knows better! Captain Sturgeon spends his time prancing around on that famous palomino of his in front of the Telly lenses, not dodging bullets. Or Ted Sohl. Colonel Ted Sohl. The dashing Sohl with his two western style six-shooters, slung low on his hips, and that romantic limp and craggy face. My, do the female buffs go for Colonel Sohl! I wonder how many of them know he wears a special pair of boots to give him that limp. Old Jerry's a long time drinking pal of mine, he's never copped one in his life. What's more, another year or so and he'll be a general and you know what that means. Almost automatic jump to Upper caste."

Joe's face was working. All this was not really news to him. Like his fellow old pros, Joe Mauser was fully aware of the glory grabbers. There had always been the glory grabbers from mythological Achilles, who sulked in his tent while his best friend died before the walls of Troy, to Alexander, who conquered the world with an army conceived and precision trained by another man whose name is all but forgotten, to the swashbuckling Custer who sacrificed self and squadron rather than wait for assistance.

Freddy pushed him. "How come you're never on lens when you're in there going good, major? Ever thought about that? When you're commanding a rear-guard action, maybe, trying to extract your lads when the situation's pickled, who's in the Telly lens where all the stupid buffs can see him? One of the manufactured heroes."

Joe scowled. "The who?"

"Come off it, major. You've been around long enough to know heroes are made, not born. We stopped having much regard for real heroes a long time ago. Lindbergh and Byrd were a couple of the last we turned out. After that, we left it to the Norwegians to do such things as crew the *Kon-Tiki*, or to the English to top Everest—whether or not the Britisher made the last hundred feet slung over the shoulder of a

Sherpa. I don't know if it was talking movies, the radio, the coming of Telly, or what. Possibly all three. But we got away from real heroes, they're not exciting enough. Telly actors can do it better. Real heroes are apt to be on the dull side, they're men who do things rather than being showmen. Actually, most adventure can be on the monotonous side, nine-tenths of the time. When a Stanley goes to find a Livingston, he doesn't spend twenty-four hours a day killing rogue elephants or fighting off tribesman; most of the time he's plodding along in the swamps, getting bitten by mosquitoes, or through the bush getting bitten by tsetse flies. So, as a people, we turned it over to the movies, and Telly, where they can do it better."

Joe Mauser's mind was working now, but he held silence.

Freddy Soligen went on, "Your typical fracas buff, glued to his Telly set, wants two things. First, lots of gore, lots of blood, lots of sadistic thrill. And the Lower-Lower lads, who are silly enough to get into the Military Category for the sake of glory or the few shares of common stock they might secure, provide that gore. Second, your Telly fan wants some Good Guys whose first requirement is to be easily recognized. Some heroes, easily identified with. Anybody can tell a Telly hero when he sees one. Handsome, dashing, distinctively uniformed, preferably tall, and preferably blond and blue-eyed, though we'll eliminate those requirements in your case, if you'll grow a mustache." He cocked his head to one side. "Yes, sir. A very dashing mustache."

Joe said sourly, "You think that's all I need to hit the big time. A dashing mustache, eh?"

"No," Freddy Soligen said, very slowly and evenly. "We're also going to need every bit of stock you've accumulated, major. We're going to have to buy your way into the columns of the fracas buff magazine. We're going to have to bribe my colleagues, the Telly camera crews, to keep you on lens when you're looking good, and, more important still, off it when you're not. We're going to have to spend every credit you've got."

"I see," Joe said. "And when it's all been accomplished, what do you get out of this, Freddy?"

Freddy Soligen laid it on the line. "When it's all been accomplished, you'll be an Upper. I'm ambitious, too, Joe. Just as ambitious as you are. I need an *In*. You'll be it. I'll make you. I have the know-how. I can do it. When you're made, you'll make me."

CHAPTER TWO

When Major Mauser, escorting Dr. Nadine Haer, daughter of the late Baron Haer of Vacuum Tube Transport, entered the swank Exclusive Room of the Greater Washington branch of the Ultra Hotels, the orchestra ceased the dreamy dance music it had been playing and struck up the lilting "The Girl I Left Behind Me."

As they followed the maître d'hôtel to their table, Nadine frowned in puzzled memory and after they were seated, she said, "That piece, where have I heard it before?"

Joe cleared his throat uncomfortably. "An old marching song, come down from way back. Popular during the Civil War. The seventh Cavalry rode forth to that tune on the way to their rendezvous with the Sioux at the Little Big Horn."

She frowned at him, puzzled still, "You seem to know an inordinate amount about a simple tune, Joe." Then she said, "Why, now I remember where I've heard it recently. Wednesday, when I was waiting for you at the Agora Bar. The band played it when you entered."

He picked up the menu, hurriedly. The Exclusive Room was ostentatious to the point of menus and waiters. "What'll you have, Nadine?" He still wasn't quite at ease with her first name. Offhand, he could never remember having been on a first name basis with a Mid-Upper, certainly not one of the female gender.

But she was not to be put off. "Why, Joe Mauser, you've acquired a theme song, or whatever you call it. I didn't know you were that well known amount the nit-wits who follow the fracases. Why next they'll be forming those ridiculous buff-clubs." Her laughter tinkled. "The Major Joe Mauser Club."

Joe flushed. "As a matter of fact, there are three," he said unhappily. "One in Mexico City, one in Bogota and one in Portland. I've forgotten if it's Oregon or Maine."

She was puzzled still, and ignored the waiter who, standing there, made Joe nervous. Establishments which boasted live waiters, were rare enough in Joe Mauser's experience that he could easily remember the number of occasions he'd attended them. Nadine Haer, to the contrary, an hereditary aristocrat born, was totally unaware of the flunky's presence and would remain so until she required him.

She looked at Joe from the side of her eyes, suspiciously. "That new mustache which gives you such a romantic air. Your new uniform, very gallant. You look like one of those Imperial Hussars or something. And your Telly interviews. By a stretch of chance, I saw one of them the other day. That master of ceremonies seemed to think you are the most dashing soldier since Jeb Stuart."

Joe said to the waiter, "Champagne, please."

That worthy said apologetically, "May I see your credit card, major? The Exclusive Room is limited to Upper—"

Nadine said coldly, "The major is my guest. I am Dr. Nadine Haer." Her voice held the patina of those to the manor born, and not to be gainsaid. The other bowed hurriedly, murmured something placatingly, and was gone.

There was a tic at the side of Joe's mouth which usually manifested itself only in combat. He said stiffly, "I am afraid we should have gone to a Middle establishment."

"Nonsense. What difference does it make? Besides, don't change the subject. I am not to be fooled, Joe Mauser. Something is afoot. Now, just what?"

The tic had intensified. Joe Mauser looked at the woman he loved, realizing that it could never occur to her that he, a Mid-Middle, would presume to think in terms of wooing her. That even in her supposed scorn of rank, privilege and status, she was still, subconsciously perhaps, a noble and he a serf. Evolution there was in society, and the terms were different, but it was still a world of class distinction and she was of the ruling class, and he the ruled, she a patrician, he a pleb.

His voice went very even, very flat, almost as though he was speaking to a foe. "When we first met, Nadine, I told you that I had been born a Mid-Lower. Why, I don't know, but from my earliest memories I revolted against the strata in which birth placed me. History—I have had lots of time to read history, in hospital beds—tells me there have been few socio-economic systems under which the strong, intelligent, aggressive, cunning or ruthless couldn't work their way to the top. Very well, I intend to do it under People's Capitalism."

"Industrial Feudalism," she murmured.

"Call it what you will. I won't be happy until I'm a member of that one per cent on top."

She looked into his face. "Are you sure you will be then?"

"I don't know," he said angrily. "But I've heard the argument before. It's been used down through the ages by apologists for the privileged classes. Pity the poor rich man. While the happy slaves are sitting down on the levee, strumming their banjos, the poor plantation owner is up in his mansion drowning his sorrows in mint juleps."

She had an edge of anger, too. "All right," she snapped. "But I'll tell you this, Joe Mauser. The world is out of gear, but the answer isn't for individuals to better their material lot by jumping their caste statuses."

The waiter brought their wine, and, both angry, both held their peace until he had served it and left.

"What *is* the answer?" he said, mock in his voice. "It's easy enough for you, on top, to tell me, below, that the answer isn't in making my way to your level."

She was interrupted in her hot reply by a rolling of the orchestra's drums and the voice of a domineering M.C. who managed effectively to drown all vocal opposition at the tables.

Grinning inanely, holding onto his portable, wireless mike, he babbled along about the wonderful people present tonight and the good time being had by all. The Exclusive Room being founded on pure snobbery, he made great todo about the celebrities present. This politician, that actress, this currently popular songstress, that baron of industry.

Joe and Nadine ignored most of his chatter, still glaring at each other, until he came to...

"And those among us who are fracas buffs, and who isn't a fracas buff these days, given the merest drop of red blood? Fracas buffs will be thrilled to know that they are spending the evening in the company of the intrepid Major Joseph Mauser..."

Behind him, the orchestra broke into the quick strains of "The Girl I Left Behind Me."

"...Whose most recent act of sheer military genius and derringdo combined resulted in his all but single-handed winning of the fracas between Continental Hovercraft and Vacuum Tube Transport, and thus inflicting defeat upon none other than Marshal Stonewall Cogswell for the first time in more than a decade."

The M.C. babbled on, now about another present celebrity, a retired pugilist, once a champion.

Nadine looked into his face. "I think I understand now. You mentioned that in any society the...how did you put it? ...the strong, intelligent, aggressive, cunning or ruthless could work their way to the top. You've tried strength, intelligence, and aggressiveness, haven't you, Joe? They didn't work. At least, not fast enough. So now you're giving cunning a try. Will ruthlessness be next, Joe Mauser?"

He was saved an answer.

A hulking body in evening wear stood next to their table, swaying. Joe looked up into a face glazed by either trank or alcohol. He didn't know the other man and for a moment failed to realize the other's purpose. The man was mumbling something that didn't come through.

Joe, irritated, said, "What in Zen do you want?"

The stranger shook his head, as though to clear it. He sneered, "The famous Joe Mauser, eh? The brave soldier-boy. Well, lemme tell you something, soldier-boy, you don't look so tough to me with your cute little mustache and your fancy-pants uniform. You look like a molly to me."

"That's too bad," Joe bit out. "And now, if you'll just go away." He turned his face from the other.

"Joe…!" Nadine said in an alarmed warning.

The other's contemptuous cuff, unsuspected, nearly bowled Joe completely from his chair. As it was, he barely caught himself.

His attacker shuffled backward and Joe recognized the trained step of the professional boxer. The other's identity now came to him, although he was no follower of pugilism, a sport largely out of favor since the rapid growth of Telly scanned fracases. Boxing at its top had never been more than an inadequate replacement of the games once held in the Roman area.

Joe was on his feet, instantly the fighting man under attack. The table that he and Nadine occupied was a ringside one, and in open view of half the room, but that meant nothing. He was under attack and for the nonce surprised, on the defensive.

"How'd you like them apples, soldier-boy?" the professional pugilist chuckled nastily. His left flicked forward and Joe barely avoided its connecting with his face.

He threw aside, for the time, any attempt to explain the other's uncalled for aggression. Unless he did something, and quick, he was going to be a laughing stock, rather than the hero into which Freddy Soligen was trying to build him.

Nadine said, Anxiously, "Joe...please...the waiters will deal with—".

He didn't hear her.

Joe Mauser, with all his hospital studies, had never heard of the Marquis of Queensbury. But even if he had, it would never have occurred to him to be bound by that arbiter of fisticuffs. In fact, he had no intention even of being restricted to the use of his hands as fists. The Japanese, long centuries before, had proven the fist less than the most effective manner in which to pursue hand-to-hand combat.

Joe Mauser, working coolly, fast and ruthlessly, now, a trained combat man exercising his profession, moved in for the kill, his shoulders hunched slightly forward, his hands forward and to the sides, choppers rather than sledges.

Joe stepped closer, as quick as a jungle cat. His left hand leapt forward to the other's neck, hacked, came back into another blurring swing, hacked again. His opponent grunted agony.

But a man does not become heavyweight champion without being able to take as well as give punishment. Joe's attacker tucked his chin into his shoulder, fighter style, and moved in throwing off the effects of the karate blows. Somehow, he seemed considerably less drunk or over-tranked than he had short moments before, and there was rage in his face, rather than glaze.

One of the blows caught Joe on a shoulder and sent him reeling back. At the same time, behind the other, Joe could see the maître d'hôtel flanked by three waiters, hurrying up. He was going to have to do something, and do it quickly, or be branded a boorish Middle who had intruded into a domain of the Uppers only to participate in a brawl and have to be expelled by the establishment's servants.

The former champ, his eyes narrowed in confidence of victory, came boring in, on his toes, quick for all of his bulk. Joe turned sideways, his movements lithe. He lashed out with his right foot, at this angle getting double the leverage he would have otherwise, and caught the other on the kneecap. The pugilist bent forward in agony, his mouth opening as though in protest.

Joe stepped forward, quickly, efficiently. His hands were now knitted together in a huge double fist. He brought them upward, crushingly, into his opponent's face, with all the force he could achieve, and felt bone and cartilage crush. Before even waiting for the other to fall, he turned, righted his chair, and resumed his seat facing Nadine, his breath coming only inconsiderably faster than before.

Her eyes were wide, but she hadn't organized herself as yet to the point of either protest or praise.

The maître d' was at their table. "Sir—" he began.

Joe said curtly, "This barroom brawler attacked me. I'm surprised you allow your patrons to get into the shape he is. Please bring our bill."

The head waiter stuttered, his eyes going about in despair, even as his assistants were lifting the fallen champion to his feet and hustling him away.

An occupant of one of the nearby tables spoke up, collaborating Joe's words. The action had been fast, though brief, and had won the fascinated attention of that half of the patrons of the Exclusive Room near enough to see. Somebody else called out, too. And it came to Joe cynically, that a brawl in an establishment exclusive to Uppers, differed little from on of Middle or even Lower caste.

But it was impossible that they remain. He had looked forward to this evening with Nadine Haer, had planned to lay the foundations for a future campaign, when, as a newly created Upper, he would be in the position to mention marriage. He fumed, inwardly, even as he helped her with her wrap, preparatory to leaving.

Nadine, now that she had recovered composure, said coldly, "I suppose you realize you broke that man's nose and injured his eye to an extent I'd have to examine him to evaluate?"

Behind her, he rolled his eyes upward in mute protest. He said, "What was I supposed to do, hand him a rose from our table bouquet?"

"Violence is the resort of the incompetent."

"You must tell that, some time, to a jungle animal being attacked by a lion."

"Oh, you're impossible!"

CHAPTER THREE

When Freddy Soligen entered his living room, he automatically switched off the Telly screen which was the entire north wall. The room's lights automatically went brighter.

His perpetual air of sour cynicism was absent as he chuckled to the room's sole inhabitant, "What! A son of mine gawking at Telly? Next I'll be finding tranks by the bowl full, sitting on the tea table."

His son grinned at him. Already, at the ago of sixteen, Samuel Soligen was a good three inches taller than his father, at least ten pounds heavier. The boy was bright of eye, toothy of smile, gawky as only a teen-ager can be gawky, and obviously the proverbial apple of his father's eye.

Sam said, the faintest note of apology in his tone, "Just finished my assignments, Papa. Thought I'd see if there was anything worthwhile on the air."

"An incurable optimist," Freddy chuckled. "You take after your mother. Believe me, Sam. There's *never* anything worthwhile on Telly."

"Not even when you're casting?"

"*Especially* when I'm casting, boy. What've you been getting at the Temple school these days? Zen! I've been so busy on a special project I've been working on, I haven't had time to keep check on whether or not you're even still living here."

The boy shrugged, picked up an apple from the sideboard and began to munch. His voice was disinterested. "Aw, Comparative Religion, mostly. We gotta go way back and study about the Greeks and the Triple-Goddess, and then the Olympians, and all that curd."

"Hey, watch your language, Sam. Remember, you're going to wind up a priest."

"Yeah," the boy grumbled, "that'll be the day. You ever heard of a Lower becoming a full priest? I'll be lucky if I ever get to monk."

Freddy Soligen sat down suddenly, across from his son, and his voice lost its edge of good-natured humor and became deadly serious. "Listen, son. You were born a High-Lower, just like your father. Unfortunately, I wasn't jumped to Low-Middle until after your birth. But you're not going to stay a High-Lower, any more than I'm going to stay a Low-Middle."

The boy shrugged, his expression almost surly, now. "Aw, what difference does it make? High-Lower isn't too bad. It's sure better than Low-Lower. I got enough stock issued me for anything I'll ever need. Or, if not, I can work a while, just like you've done, and earn a few more shares."

Freddy Soligen's face worked, in alarm. "Hey, Sam, listen here. We've been over this before, but may be not as thoroughly as we should've. Sure, this is People's Capitalism and on top of that the Welfare State; they got all sorts of fancy names to call it. You've got cradle to the grave security. Instead of waiting for old age, or thirty years of service, or something, to get your pension, it starts at birth. At long last, the jerks have inherited the earth."

The boy said plaintively, as though in objection to his father's sneering words. "You aren't talking against the government, or the old time way of doing things, are you Papa? What's wrong with what we got? Everybody's got it made. Nobody hasta—".

His father was impatiently waving a hand at him in negation. "No, everybody doesn't have it made. Almost everybody's bogged down. That's the trouble Sam. The guts have been taken out of us. And ninety-nine people out of a hundred don't care. They've got bread and butter security. They've got trank to keep them happy. And they've got the fracases to watch, the sadistic, gory death of others to keep them amused, and their minds off what's really being done to them. We're not part of that ninety-nine out of a hundred, Sam. We're two of those who aren't jerks. We're on our way up out of the mob, to where life can be full. Got it, son? A full life. Doing things worth doing. Thinking things worth thinking. Associating with people who have it on the ball."

He had come to his feet in his excitement and was pacing before the boy who sat now, mouth slightly agape at his father's emphasis.

"Sam, listen. I'm getting along. Already in my forties, and I never did get much education when I was young. Maybe I'll never make it but you can. That's why I insisted you switch categories. You were born into Communications, like me, but switched to Religion. Why'd you think I wanted that?"

"Aw, I don't know, Papa. I thought maybe—".

His father snorted. "Look, son, I haven't spent as much time with you as I should. Especially since your mother left us. She just couldn't stand what she called my being against everything. She was one of the jerks, Sam—".

"You oughtn'ta talk about my mother that way," Sam said sullenly.

"All right, all right. I just meant that she was willing to spend her life sucking on trank, watching Telly, and living on the pittance income from the unalienable stock shares issued her at birth. But let's get to this religious curd. Son, whatever con man first thought up the idea of gods put practically the whole human race on the sucker list. You say they're giving you comparative religion in your classes at the Temple now, eh? O.K., have you ever heard of a major religion where the priests didn't do just fine for themselves?"

"But Papa... Well, shucks, there's always been—"

"Certainly, certainly, individuals. Crackpots, usually, out of tune with the rest of the priesthood. But the rank and file do pretty well for themselves. Didn't you point out earlier that a Lower, in our society, never makes full priest? Not to speak of bishop, or ultra-bishop. They're Uppers, part of the ruling hierarchy."

"Well, what's all this got to do with me getting into Category Religion? I'd think it'd be more fun in Communications, like you. Gee, Papa, going around meeting all those famous—"

Freddy Soligen's face worked. "Look, son. Sure, I meet lots of people on top. But the thing is, eventually you're going to become one of those people, not just interview them." He began pacing again in nervous irritation.

"Sam, those on top want to stay there. Like always. They freeze things so they, and their kids, will remain on top. In our case, they've made it all but impossible for anybody to progress from the caste they were born in. Not impossible, but almost. They've got to allow for the man with extraordinary ability, like, to bust out to the top, if he's got it on the ball. Otherwise, there'd be an explosion."

"That's not the way they say in school."

"It sure isn't. The story is that anybody can make Upper-Upper if he has the ability. But the thing is, Sam, you can't make a jerk realize he's a jerk. If he sees somebody else rise in caste, he can't see why he shouldn't. That's why real rising has been restricted to Category Military and Category Religion. In the military, a man gives up his security, obviously, and if he's a jerk he dies.

"In Category Religion they've got another way to sort out the jerks and make sure they never get further than monk and beyond the caste of High-Lower. Gods always work in mysterious ways and anybody in Category Religion who doesn't have faith in the wisdom of the God's mysterious choices of who to ordain and who to reject, obviously shows that he's not really got the *true faith* which is, of course, essential to a priest, not to speak of bishop or ultra-bishop. So obviously, the Gods were wise in rejecting him. In simpler words, the would-be priest who simply hasn't got what it takes, can be given the heave-ho without it being necessary for him, or his family or friends, to understand why. It's all very simple; he lacked the humility essential in a priest of the Gods, as proven by his rebellious reaction."

Sam said, unhappily, "I don't get all this."

Freddy Soligen came to a pause before the boy, sat down again abruptly and patted his son's knee. "You're young, Sam. Too young to understand some of it. Trust your father. Stick to your studies now. You have to get the basic gobbledygook. But you're on your way up the ladder, son. I've got a deal cooking that's going to give us an in. Can't tell you about it now, but it'll mean an important break for us."

It was then that the door announced, "Major Joseph Mauser, calling on Fredric Soligen."

CHAPTER FOUR

Joe Mauser shook hands with the Telly reporter in an abrupt, impatient manner.

Freddy said, "Major, I'd like to introduce my son, Samuel. Sam, this is Major Joe Mauser. You don't follow the fracases, but the major's one of the best mercenaries in the field."

Sam scrambled to his feet and shook hands. "Gee, Joe Mauser."

Joe looked at him questioningly. "I thought you didn't follow the fracases."

Sam grinned awkwardly. "Well, gee, you can't miss picking up some stuff about the fighting. All the other guys are buffs."

Joe said to Freddy, "Could I speak to you alone?"

"Certainly, certainly. Sam, run along the major and I have business."

When the boy was gone, Joe sank into a chair and looked up at the Telly reporter accusingly. He said, "This fancy uniform, I stood still for. That idea of picking a song to identify me with and bribing the orchestra leaders to swing into it whenever I enter some restaurant or nightclub, might have its advantages. Getting me all sorts of Telly interviews, between fracases, and all those write-ups in the fracas buff magazines, I can see the need for, in spite of what it's costing. But what in Zen..." His voice went dangerous. "...was the idea of sticking that punch-drunk prizefighter on me in the most respectable nightclub in Greater Washington?"

Freddy grinned ruefully. "Oh, you figured that out, eh?"

"Did you think I was stupid?"

Freddy rubbed his hands together, happily. "He used to be world champion, and you flattened him. It was in every gossip column in the country, every news reporter, played it up. And hell all it cost us was five shares of your Vacuum Tube Transport stock."

"Five shares!"

"Why not? He used to be champ. Now, he's so broke he's got to live on stock he isn't allowed to sell. His basic government issue at birth. He was willing to take a dive cheap, if you ask me."

Joe growled at him unhappily. "I've got news for you, Freddy. Your hired brawler started off as per instructions, evidently, but after a couple of blows had been exchanged his slap-happy brain lost the message and he tried to take me. We're lucky he didn't splatter me all over the dance floor of the Exclusive Club. He didn't take a dive. I had to scuttle him."

Freddy blinked. "Zen!"

"Sure, sure, sure," Joe growled. "Look, next time you decide to spend five shares of my stock on some deal like this, let me know, eh?"

Freddy walked to the sideboard and got glasses. "Whiskey?" he said.

"Tequila, if you've got it," Joe said. "Look, I'm beginning to have second thoughts about this campaign. Where's it got us, so far?"

Freddy brought the fiery Mexican drink and handed it to him, and took a place in the chair opposite. His voice went persuasive. "It's going fine. You're on everybody's lips. First thing you know, some of the armaments firms will be having you indorse their guns, swords, cannon, or whatever."

"Oh, great," Joe growled. "Already my friends are ribbing me about this fancy uniform and all the plugs I've been getting. The glory-grabber isn't any more popular today among real pros than he's ever been."

"Who gives a damn?" Freddy sneered, cynically. "We're not in this to please your lame-brain mercenary pals with their soldier-of-fortune codes of behavior. We're in this for Number One, Joe Mauser, and Number Two, Freddy Soligen."

Joe put away the greater part of his drink. "Sure, sure, sure. But where are we now? Your campaign has been in full swing for months. What's accomplished?"

The small Telly reporter was indignant. "What's accomplished? We've got three Major Joe Mauser buff clubs in full swing and five more starting up. And next month you're going to be on the cover of the *Fracas Times*."

"And I'm still a major and still Mid-Middle caste. And my stock shares available for bribery are running short."

Freddy twisted his mouth and looked worriedly down into his glass. He said unhappily, "We need a gimmick to climax all this. Some kind of gimmick to bring you absolutely to the top."

"A gimmick?" Joe demanded. "What do you mean, a gimmick?"

"You're going to have to do something really spectacular. Make you the biggest Telly hero of them all. We'll have to get you into a real fracas and pull something dramatic. I don't know what, I don't seem to be able to come up with an angle. But when I do, I'll guarantee that every Telly camera covering the fracas will be zeroed in on Joe Mauser."

"Great," Joe growled. "I've got just the gimmick. It'll wow them."

The Telly reported looked up, hopefully.

"I'll get killed in a burst of glory," Joe said.

CHAPTER FIVE

A servant took Joe Mauser's cap at the door and requested that Joe follow him. Joe trailed behind on the way to the living room of the mansion, somewhat taken aback by the, to him, ostentation of the display of the luxuries of yesteryear. Among them was to be numbered the butler. Servants, other than military batmen, were simply not in Joe's world. Only the Uppers were in position to utilise the full time of individuals. Long years past, those tasks which once called for servants had been automated, from automated elevators to automated baby-sitters.

The servant announced him and then seemingly disappeared in the brief moment while Joe was bowing formally over Nadine Haer's hand. Even while murmuring the appropriate banalities, Joe wondered how one acquired the ability to seemingly disappear, once one's services were no longer needed. Each man to his own trade, he decided.

He had a date with Nadine, but it turned out that the piquant Upper was not alone. In fact, it was obvious that she had not as yet got around to dressing for her appointment with Joe. He had promised to take her soaring in his sailplane. She was attired, as always, as those dress who have never considered the cost of clothing. And, as ever, when Joe saw her newly, after a period of a day or more away, he was taken with her intensity and her almost brittle beauty. What was it that the aristocrat seemed able to acquire after but a generation or two of what they were pleased to call breeding? That aloof quality, the exquisite gentility.

"Joe," Nadine said, "you'll be pleased to meet Philip Holland, Category Government, Rank Secretary. Phil, Major Joseph Mauser."

The other, possibly forty, shook hands firmly and looked into Joe's face. He had a crisp manner. "Good heavens, yes," he said. "That remarkable innovation of using an engineless aircraft for reconnaissance. My old friend, Marshal Cogswell, was speaking of it the other day. I assume that in advance you purchased stock in the firms which manufacture such craft, major. They must be booming."

Joe grimaced wryly. "No, sir. I wasn't smart enough to think of that. Professional soldiers are traditionally stupid. What was the old expression? They can take their shirts off without unbuttoning their collars."

Philip Holland cocked his head, even as he chuckled. "I detect a note of bitterness, major."

Nadine said airily, "Joe is ambitious, thinking the answer to all his problems lies in jumping his caste to Upper."

Joe looked at her impatiently to where she sat on a Mid-Twentieth Century type sofa.

Philip Holland said, "Possibly he's right, my dear. Each of us have different needs to achieve such happiness as is possible to man."

To Joe, he sounded just vaguely on the stuffy side, even through the crispness. By nature nervous and quick moving, Holland seemed to try and project an air of calm which didn't quite come off. Joe wondered what his relationship to Nadine could be, a twinge of jealousy there. But that was ridiculous. Nadine must be in the vicinity of thirty. Obviously, she knew, and had known, many men as attracted to her as was Joe Mauser—And men in her own caste, at that. Somehow, though, he felt Holland was no Upper. The other simply didn't have the air.

Joe said to him, "Nadine doesn't get my point. I contend that in a strata divided society, it's hard to realize yourself fully until you're a member of the upper caste. Admittedly, perhaps you won't even if you are such a member, but at least you haven't the obstacles with which the lower class or classes are beset."

"Interestingly stated," Holland said briskly. He returned to his chair from which he had arisen to shake hands with

Joe, and looked at Nadine. "You said, on introducing us, that Joe would be glad to meet me, my dear. Why, especially?"

Nadine laughed. "Because I have been practicing your arguments upon him."

Both of the men frowned at her.

Nadine looked at Joe. "Phil Holland's the most interesting man I know, I do believe. He's secretary to Marlow Mannerheim, the Minister of Foreign Affairs, and simply couldn't be more privy to the inner workings of government. It was Phil who convinced me that something is wrong with our socio-economic system."

"Oh?" Joe said. He wasn't really interested. Let society solve its problems. He had his own. And they were sufficient unto themselves as well as the day thereof. However, conversation was to be kept moving. He needled the other. "I've heard it contended that any type of government is good given capable, intelligent personnel to run it, or bad if not so managed. What was the example I read somewhere? Both heaven and hell are despotisms."

Phil Holland shrugged. "An interesting observation. However, institutions, including socio-political ones, can become outdated. When they do, no matter how intelligent, capable and honest the governmental heads, that socio-political system can be a hell. If, at such time there are capable, intelligent persons available, they will take such measures as are necessary to change the institutions."

Nadine had come to her feet. "The subject is my favorite, but I must change. Joe is taking me a-gliding, and I'm sure this frock isn't *de rigueur.* You gentlemen will excuse me?" She was off before they had time to come to their feet.

Joe Mauser settled himself again, crossing his legs. He said, idly, "And you think our basic institutions have reached the state of needing change?"

"Perhaps, although as a member of the Government Category, it should hardly be my position to advocate such." He seemed to switch subjects. "Have you read much of the Roman *ludi*, the games as we call them?"

"The gladiators and such?" Joe shrugged. "I've read a bit about them. It's been pointed out, in fact by Dr. Haer, among others, that basically our present day fracases serve the same purposes. That instead of bread and circuses, provided by the Roman patricians to keep the unemployed Roman mob from becoming restive, we give them trank pills and Telly violence."

"Um-m-m," Holland nodded, "but that isn't the point I was making right now. What I was thinking was that at first the Roman games were athletic affairs without bloodshed. It wasn't until 264 B.C. that three pairs of slaves were sent in to fight with swords. By 183 B.C. the number had gone up to sixty pairs. By 145 B.C. ninety pairs fought for three days. But that was just the beginning. They really got under way with the dictators. Sulla put a hundred lions into the arena, but Julius Caesar topped that with four hundred and Pompey that with six hundred, plus over four hundred leopards and twenty elephants. Augustus beat them all with three thousand five hundred elephants and ten thousand men killed in a series of games. But it was the emperors who really expanded the ludi. Trajan had ten thousand animals killed in the arena to celebrate his victory over the Dacians, not to mention eleven thousand people.

"Are you surprised at my memory? The subject has always fascinated me. For one thing, I am a great believer in the theory that history repeats itself. As time went on, arenas were built all over the empire, even small towns boasted their own. In Rome, the number of them grew so that eventually an avid follower could attend every day, the year around. And as they increased in quantity they also had to grow more extreme to hold the fan's attention. The Emperor Philip, in celebrating the thousandth anniversary of the founding of Rome, had killed a thousand pair of gladiators, a rhinoceros, six hippopotami, ten hyenas, ten giraffes, twenty wild asses, ten tigers, ten zebras, thirty leopards, sixty lions, thirty-two elephants, forty wild horses. I am afraid I forgot the rest."

Joe stirred in his chair. The other's personality grew on him. The crisp voice had a certain magnetic quality that made what he said important, somehow. However, Joe's interest in Roman history wasn't exactly paramount.

Holland said, "You wonder at what I am driving, eh? Do you realize the expense involved in getting a rhinoceros to Rome in those days? Not to speak of hippopotami, tigers, lions and leopards. Few people realize the extent to which the Romans went to acquire exotic animals to be slaughtered for the edification of the mob. They penetrated as far south as Kenya, there are still the ruins of a Roman fort there; as far east as Indonesia; as far north as the Baltic, and there is even evidence that they brought polar bears from Iceland."

Philip Holland snorted, as though in contempt. "But the mob wearied of even such spectacle as giraffes being killed by pigmies from the Iturbi forest. The games had started as fights between skilled swordsmen, being observed by knowledgeable combat soldiers of a warrior people. But as the Romans lost their warlike ardor and became a worthless mob performing no useful act for either themselves or the State, they no longer appreciated a drawn-out duel between equals. They wanted quick blood, and lots of it, and turned to mass slaughter of Christians, runaway slaves, criminals and whoever else they could find to throw to the lions, crocodiles or whatever. Even this became old hat, and they turned increasingly to more extreme sadism. Children were hung up by their heels and animals turned loose to pull them down.

Men were tied face to face with rotting corpses and so remained until death. Animals were taught to rape virgins."

Joe Mauser stirred again. What in Zen was this long monologue on the Roman games leading to?

Holland said, "By the way, contrary to some belief, the games didn't end upon Christianity becoming the dominant faith and finally the State religion. Constantine legalized Christianity in 313 A.D. but it wasn't until 365 that Valentinian passed a law against sacrificing humans to animals in the arena and the gladiator schools remained in operation until 399. The arenas were finally closed in 404 A.D. but by that time the Roman Empire was a mockery. In all they last more than half a millennium, but things move faster these days."

The tone of voice changed abruptly and Holland snapped a question at Joe. "By your age, I would imagine you've participated in the present day fracases for some fifteen years. How have they changed in that time?"

Joe was taken aback. "Why..." he said, hesitated as he got the other's point, then went on, nodding. "Yes. They used to be company size—a few hundred lads involved. After a while, a battalion size fracas became fairly commonplace, then about ten years ago a corporation of any size had to be able to put at least a regiment into the field and the biggies had brigades."

"And now?" Holland urged.

"Now a divisional size fracas is the thing."

"Yes, and if a corporation isn't among the top dozen or so, a single defeat can mean bankruptcy."

Joe nodded. He had known of such cases.

Holland leaned back in his chair, as though all his points had been made. He said, his voice less brisk, "Our People's Capitalism, our Welfare State, took the road of bringing the equivalent of the Roman ludi to keep our people in a state of stupefied acceptance of the *status quo*. And as in the case of Rome, the games are bankrupting it. Our present day patrician class, our Uppers, have a tiger by the tail, Joseph Mauser, and can't let go. We need those capable and intelligent people of whom you spoke earlier, to make some basic changes. Where are they? Nadine said that your great driving ambition is to be jumped to Upper in caste. But even though you make it, what will you have on your hands but these problems that the Uppers seem unable to solve?"

Joe said, impatiently, "Possibly you're right. What you say about the fracases becoming bigger and more expensive is true. They're also becoming more bloody. In the old days, a corporation or union going into a fracas was conscious of having a high casualty list among the mercenaries. Highly trained soldiers cost money. Insurance, indemnity, pensions, all the rest of it. Consequently, you'd fight a battle of movement, maneuver, brainwork on the part of the officer commanding, so that practically nobody was hurt on either side. One force or the other would surrender after being caught in an impossible situation. Not any more. These days, they want blood. Plenty of blood. And they want the Telly cameras to focus right into the middle of it."

Joe shook his head. "But it's not my problem to solve. I've got my goal. I'll worry about other ones when I've achieved it."

A voice behind him said superciliously, "I do believe it's the status hungry captain, ah, that is, major these days. To what do I owe this unexpected visit, Major Mauser?"

Joe came to his feet and faced the newcomer, Philip Holland doing the same, somewhat more leisurely.

Baron Balt Haer, wearing a colonel's uniform and flicking his swagger stick along his booted leg, stood in the doorway. His voice was lazily arrogant. "And Mr. Holland, I must say, the Middle caste seems to have taken over the house. Well,

Major Mauser? I assume you do not labor under the illusion that you are welcome in this dwelling."

In Category Military rank is observed whilst in uniform, even though neither individual is currently on active service. Joe had automatically come to attention. He said, stiffly, "Sir, I am calling upon your sister, Dr. Haer."

"Indeed," Baron Haer said, his nostrils high in that attitude once perfected by grandees of medieval Spain, landed gentry of England, Prussian Junkers. "I find that my sister, in her capacity as medical scientist, seems to go to extreme in her research. What aspect of the lower classes is she studying in your case, major?"

Joe flushed. "Baron Haer," he said, "we seem to have got off on the wrong foot when we participated in that fracas against Continental Hovercraft under your father, the late Baron. I would appreciate an opportunity to start over again."

"Would you indeed?" Balt Haer said loftily. He turned his eye to Philip Holland, whose mouth bore the slightest suggestions of suppressed humor. "Unless I am mistaken, the conversation at the time of my entry seemed to have a distinctly subversive element. Shouldn't this be somewhat surprising in the secretary of the administration's foreign minister?"

Philip Holland said crisply, "You must have intruded, um-m-m, that is, entered, at the end of a sentence, Baron Haer. We were merely discussing the various methods, down through the ages, that ruling classes have utilized to perpetuate themselves in power."

Haer obviously disbelieved him. He said, "For example?"

"There are many examples," Holland said, reseating himself. "For instance, the medieval feudalistic class who dominated the ignorant and highly superstitious serfdom soon found it expedient to add to their titles *by grace of God*, as though it was God's wish that they be count or baron, prince or king. What serf would dare attempt the overthrow of his lord, in the face of God's wishes?"

"I see," Balt Haer said. "And other examples?"

Holland shrugged. "The Chinese Mandarins utilized possibly the most unique method of a governing class perpetuating itself ever known, certainly one of the most gentle."

Haer was scowling at him, obviously out of his depth, as was Joe Mauser for that matter.

Holland said crisply, "The mandarins devised a written language so complicated that it took at least ten years to master reading and writing, thus assuring that only the very well-to-do could afford to educate their sons. When invaded, as so often China has been invaded, only the mandarins were in the position to serve the conquerors by carrying on the paperwork so vital to any advanced society. So, still in control of the machinery of government, they continued to perpetuate themselves, and shortly—as history is reckoned—we found the conquerors assimilated and the mandarins still in power."

Balt Haer said impatiently, "I seem to be under the impression that you were speaking of more current times, when I entered, Mr. Holland."

From the door, Nadine said, "Good heavens, Balt, are you badgering my guests again?"

The three men faced her.

Balt said nastily, "I am astonished that you persist in bringing members of the lower orders into my home, Nadine."

"Our home, Balt. In fact, if you must bring up such matters before outsiders, you will recall that you converted your portion of the family estate into continental Hovercraft stock, shortly before father met Baron Zwerdling's forces in the recent fracas. No wonder you dislike Major Mauser. Through his efforts, our company won, rather than losing as you had expected."

Her brother, who could have been only slightly her senior, was obviously enraged. "Are you suggesting that I am not welcome to stay in this, our family home, simply because the property is in your name?"

"Not at all," she sighed. "You are always at home here, Balt, I simply demand that you exercise common courtesy to my guests."

He turned and walked stiff kneed from the room.

"Sorry," Joe said to Nadine.

"Why?" she said simply. "The fact of the matter is that Balt and I are continually at each other. He is quite the active member of the Nathan Hale society."

Joe frowned his ignorance and looked at Holland.

Holland chuckled. "An ultra-conservative—reactionary might be the better term—organization devoted to witch hunting and such in its efforts to maintain the *status quo*, major. Once again, history repeats itself. Such groups invariably evolve when basic change threatens a socio-economic system." He looked at Nadine. "I must be going, my dear. My, how charming you look. If this is the customary garb whilst going a-gliding, I shall have to take up the sport."

"Why Phil, inane words of flattery from serious old you?"

Joe squirmed inwardly, wondering again upon what basis was the friendship of Nadine Haer and Philip Holland.

The butler entered and said, "A call for Major Mauser, if you please."

Only Max Mainz, his batman during his last fracas and now permanently attached to Joe, knew that he might be found at this address. Joe said to Nadine, "Would you pardon me for a moment? I assume it's something important, or I wouldn't be disturbed."

She said, demurely, "Undoubtedly one of the feminine members of a Joe Mauser buff club."

He snorted amusement and followed the butler to the library and the tele-screen.

Max Mainz's face loomed in the viewing screen. As soon as Joe appeared, he said, "Major, sir, the marshal's been trying to get hold of you ever since you left the hotel."

"The marshal?" Joe scowled.

"Marshal Cogswell. That one they call Stonewall Cogswell. And when he wants somebody, he really wants 'em, and I got a feeling it's a good idea to come on the double."

Joe laughed. "Stonewall Cogswell's a tough one all right, Max."

"You ain't just a countin' down, major, sir. He says when I get hold of you to come on over to his headquarters soonest."

"All right, Max, thanks." Joe flicked the set off.

Actually, Max was right. You didn't ignore a summons from Marshal Cogswell. Not if you were in the Category Military and ambitious. The date with Nadine was off. And just when he was beginning to detect signs of her meeting him on his own level.

CHAPTER SIX

It was the common practice among Category Military mercenaries of highest rank to maintain skeleton staffs between those periods when they were under hire by corporations or unions. That of Marshal Stonewall Cogswell was one of the most complete, he habitually keeping upward of a hundred officers in his private uniform. It paid off, for with such a skeleton force of highly skilled professionals as a cadre, the marshal could enlist veterans for his rank and file and whip together a trained fighting force in a fantastically short period.

And nothing was so of the essence as time, in the present Category Military. For when two corporations sued for permission to meet on a military reservation for trial by combat to settle their commercial differences, the sums involved were staggering. Joe Mauser had been correct in saying that the fracas had grown, even in his memory, from skirmishes involving a company or two of men, to full fledged battles with a division or even more on either side, forty thousand men at each other's throats.

So a commanding officer became noted not only for his abilities in the field, but also those of cutting financial corners, recruiting his force of mercenaries, whipping them into a unit and getting them into the action. In fact, corporations, these days, invariably stated the period of time to be involved when they petitioned the Category Military Department. Perhaps a month, three weeks of which would be used for recruiting and drill, the last week for the fracas itself. Nobody could excel Marshal Cogswell in using the three weeks to best advantage.

Major Joe Mauser came to attention before the desk of the lieutenant colonel of Marshal Cogswell's staff who was acting as receptionist before the sanctum sanctorum of the field genius. He saluted and snapped, "Joseph Mauser, sir. Category Military, Rank Major. On request to see the marshal."

Lieutenant Colonel Paul Warren answered the salute, but then came to his feet and grinned while extending his hand to be shaken. He said, "Good to see you again, Mauser. Hope you're in this one with us." His grin turned rueful. "That trick of yours with the glider cost me a pretty penny. I'd made the mistake of wagering heavily on Hovercraft. But the marshal is waiting. Right through that door, major. See you later."

Evidently, Joe decided, the marshal was recruiting for another fracas. Which was why Joe had been summoned, although when a field officer of Cogswell's stature was gathering officers to command a force, he seldom called upon them; they clamored for permission to serve with him. You weren't apt to find yourself in the dill, under Cogswell, and you practically never failed to collect your victory bonus. Victory was a habit.

Marshal Cogswell looked up from the desk at which he sat scowling at a military chart stretched before him. The scowl disappeared and his strong face lit with pleasure. The craggy marshal was a small man but strongly built, clipped of voice and with a tone that would suggest he had been born to command, had always commanded.

Joe snapped to the salute which the marshal acknowledged with a flick of his baton, then stood to shake hands. "Ah, Major Mauser. Bit of trouble locating you." His eyes narrowed momentarily. "Trust you are not at present affiliated with any company colors." He took in Joe's uniform and scowled vaguely, not placing it.

Joe said in self-deprecation, "This is my own devising, sir. I thought if I was going to have to present myself to be killed, for a living, that I might as well show up before the screens as distinctively as possible. I've been told that ultimately the fracas buffs make or break you, in our category."

The marshal frowned, as though unhappy and possibly surprised at Joe's words, however, he sat down again and repeated his question by merely looking at the other.

"No, sir, I'm free," Joe said. "However, frankly, I wasn't looking for a commission right at this time."

Cogswell stared at him. Mauser was a good junior officer and they'd been through half a dozen fracases together over the years, not always on the same side.

"Why not?" Cogswell barked. "Are you convalescing, major? Surely you didn't manage to cop one in that last farce?"

"Personal reasons, sir."

"Very well," Cogswell growled. "However, I'm going to attempt to sway you, major. Would seem that I am up against it, if I don't, and, in a manner it's your fault."

Joe was bewildered. "My fault, sir?"

The older man's voice went brisk. "This is the situation. I have been approached by the United Miners to command their forces in their trial by combat with Carbonaceous Fuel. Same old issues, of course. Contract between the union and corporation is usually for only two years. Each time it comes up again, the union officials try to get a larger cut of the pie and the hereditary heads of Carbonaceous Fuel resist. Automatically, the Category Military Department issues a permit. The fracases they've been fighting prove so popular that there'd be riots if the permit was refused. Frankly, I'm no great admirer of the group in control of United Miners, but—"

Joe was surprised enough to say, "Why not, sir?" Old pro mercenaries seldom concerned themselves as to the issues or principles involved in a fracas. They chose their side by more mundane considerations.

Marshal Cogswell looked at him testily. "Sit down, Joe. You're not on my staff, as yet, at least. Zen take the formality!" When Joe had accepted the chair, he growled again. "Suppose you didn't know I was born into Category Mining?"

"No, sir."

"Well, I was. But even as a boy this new industrial revolution was cutting the number of employees involved in the category each year that went by."

"That's happened in every field, sir. Including my original one." Joe Mauser was thinking, *so what?*

"Of course," Cogswell rapped. "My objection is what happened to the union. Unions were originally founded as an instinctive gathering together of employees to achieve as high a pay as they could get from the employer, with the strike as their weapon. But whatever the original purpose, and its virtue or lack of it, the union grew into something entirely different by the early and middle twentieth century. Such unions as the United Miners grew to such a size that they, themselves, became some of the largest business organizations in the country. And eventually they came to be run, like any other business, for the benefit of those who owned or controlled them. The professional labor leader evolved, motivated by his own interests and finally becoming, in his despotic control of the union, backed by goon squads and gangsters, as powerful a man as was to be found in the country. Seldom were strikes any longer held to better the condition of the individual union members. Instead, the issues were contracts which allowed for fabulous sums to go into the union coffers where they were at the disposal of the union officials."

The marshal grunted sourly. "Now that the whole industry of mining is all but completely automated and only a few thousands employed actively, there are confounded few miners not on the unemployed list, but the union officials wax as fat as ever, what with the percentages of each ton mined going into so-called welfare funds, and such."

He looked at Joe, evidently conscious that he had made an inordinary long speech for the supposedly taciturn Stonewall Cogswell. He cleared his throat and said, "Not that it's my affair. I switched categories to Military, in my youth. Let us get to the point. I've been caught napping, Joe."

That was an unlooked for confession to come from Stonewall Cogswell. Joe said nothing, waiting for more.

The marshal shook his baton at the younger officer. "By utilizing that confounded glider of yours as a reconnaissance craft, you revolutionized present warfare, major. Act of absolute ingenuity, and I admired it. Unfortunately, I failed to realize the speed with which every professional in our category would jump upon the bandwagon and secure gliders for himself."

Joe saw light.

"Been caught short," Cogswell rapped. "Short of gliders. Short of even one glider. And within a few weeks I'm committed to a divisional size fracas." He pushed back his chair, angrily. "General McCord is in command of the Carbonaceous Fuel forces. Met him before, and always brought up victory only by the skin of my teeth. But this time he has two gliders. I have none."

"But, sir, surely you can either buy or rent several craft on the market."

"Confound it! It's not the machines that are unavailable, but the trained pilots to operate them. The sport hasn't been popular in half a century. Not overly so, even then."

"But training a pilot—"

"Training a pilot, nonsense!" the marshal was shaking his baton at him again, in indignation. "A *pilot* won't do. He must also be a trained reconnaissance man. Must be able to follow terrain from the air. Identify military forces both in nature and number. I needn't tell you this, major. You above all know the problem."

It hadn't occurred to Joe, but the other was obviously right. There couldn't be more than a few dozen men in Category Military who could hold down both the job of pilot and reconnaissance officer. In another six months, the situation would have changed. Officers would quickly be trained. But now? As Cogswell said, he was caught short.

Joe came to his feet. "Sir, I'll have to consider the commission. Frankly, my plans were otherwise."

Cogswell started at him grimly. "Mauser, you've always been one of the best. An old pro, in every sense of the word. However, there have been some rumors going around about your ambitions."

Joe said stiffly, "Sir, my ambitions are my own business, whatever these rumors."

"Didn't say I believed them, major. We've been together too often when the situation has pickled for me to judge you without more evidence than gossip. What I was leading up to, is this. There's nothing wrong with ambition. If you see me through in this, I'll do what I can toward pushing your promotion."

Joe came to the salute again. "Thank you, sir. I'll consider the commission and let you know by tomorrow."

Cogswell flicked the baton, in his nonchalant answer to salute. "That will be all, then, major."

CHAPTER SEVEN

Freddy Soligen wasn't at home when Joe Mauser called. The Category Military officer was met, instead, by young Sam Soligen, clothed this day in the robes of a novitiate of the Temple. Joe remembered now that Freddy had mentioned the boy in training in Category Religion.

Sam led him back into the living room, switching off the Telly screen which had been tuned in on one of the fictionalized fracases of the past. Poor entertainment, when compared to the real thing, for any fracas buff, but better than nothing. In fact, it was even contended by some that if you got yourself properly tranked you could get almost as much emotion from a phony-fracas, as they were called, as for the genuine.

"Gee, sir," Sam said, "Papa was supposed to be back by now. I don't know where he is. If you wanta wait—"

Joe shrugged and picked himself a chair. He took in Sam's robes and made conversation. "Studies tough in the Temple schools?" he asked.

The teen-ager realized it was a make-talk question. He said, "Aw, not much. A lot of curd about rituals and all. You hafta memorize it."

"Curd, yet," Joe laughed. "You don't sound particularly pious, Sam. Come to think of it, I suppose any child of Freddy's could hardly be."

Sam said, his young voice urgent, "Papa said you were on your way up, Major Mauser. Just like us. Gee, how come you chose Category Military, instead of Religion?"

Joe Mauser looked at the other. It was his policy to treat young people either as children or adults. If he was to deal with a teen-ager as an adult, he didn't believe in pulling punches any more than had he been dealing with a person of sixty. He said, flatly, "I've never had much regard for those categories in which a man makes his living battening on human sorrow or fear, Sam. That includes in my book such fields as religion, undertakers and their affiliates, and even most doctors, for that matter." He added, to explain the last inclusion, "They profit too much from illness, for my satisfaction."

Major Mauser was enough of a current celebrity for practically anything he said to be impressive to young Sam Soligen. That youngster blinked. He said, "Well, gee, don't you believe in any gods at all? If you believe in any god at all, you gotta have a religious category, and that means priests."

"Why?" Joe said. Inwardly, he was amused at himself for getting into a debate with this youngster and even a trifle ashamed of needling the boy about his chosen field. But he said, "If there are gods, I doubt if they'd intrust a priesthood to threaten their created humanity with hellfire."

Sam was taken aback. "Well, why not?"

"Gods couldn't be bothered with such triviality. In fact, I'd think it unlikely they could be bothered with priests. If I was a god, certainly I couldn't."

The boy's face was intent, its youthfulness somewhat ludicrous in view of the dark robes he wore. He leaned forward, "Yeah, you talk about priests and undertakers and all battening on human sorrow, but how about you? How about the Category Military? How many men you killed, major?"

Joe winced. "Too many," he said abruptly. The tic was at the side of his mouth, unbeknownst to him. He added, "But mercenaries have deliberately chosen their path. They know what they're going into and they do it willingly, they haven't been drafted."

He thought a moment, and Phil Holland's talk about the Roman *ludi* came back to him. He said, "It's like the difference between throwing a bunch of Christians to some wild bulls in a Roman arena, to being a torero in Spain, a matador who has chosen his profession and enters the bullring to make money."

Then the boy said something that gave him greater depth than Joe had expected. "Yeah," he said, "but maybe the torero was forced into becoming a bullfighter on account of how bad he needed the money." In the heat of the discussion, he was emboldened to add, "And these new Rank Privates that go into a fracas, not knowing what it's all about, just filled with all the stuff we see on Telly and all. How much of a chance does one of them have if he runs into an old-timer like Joe Mauser, out there in no-man's-land?"

Touché, Joe thought.

There was the action that sometimes came back to him in his dreams. He had been a sergeant then, but already the veteran of five years or more standing, and a double score of fracases. The force of which he was a member had been in full retreat, and Joe's squad was part of the rear-guard. The terrain had been mountainous, the High Sierra Military Reservation. Four of his men had copped one, two so badly that they had to be left behind, incapable of being moved. Joe, under the pressure of long hours of retreat under fire, had finally sent the others on back, and found himself a crevice, near the top of a sierra, which was all but impregnable.

His rifle had been a .45-70 Springfield, with its ultra-heavy slug, but slow muzzle velocity. And Joe had a telescope mounted upon it, an innovation that barely made the requirement of predating the year 1900 and thus subscribing to the Universal Disarmament Pact between the Sov-world and the West-world. It had taken the enemy forces a long time to even locate him, a long time and half a dozen casualties that Joe had coolly inflicted. The way to get to him, the only way, involved exposure. Joe could see the enemy officers, through his scope, at a distance just out of his range. They knew the situation, being old pros. He found considerable satisfaction in the rage he knew they were feeling. He was dominating a considerable section of the front, due to the terrain, and there was but one way to root him out, direct frontal attack.

They had sent in Rank Privates; Low-Lowers, most of them in their first fracas. Low-Lowers, the dregs of society, seldom employed and then at the rapidly disappearing, all but extinct, unskilled labor jobs. Low-Lowers, most of them probably in this fracas in hopes of the unlikelihood of so distinguishing themselves that they would be jumped a caste, or at least acquire an extra share or two of common stock to better the basic living guaranteed by the State. Rank Privates, most in their first fracas, unknowledgeable about taking cover and not even in the physical condition this sort of combat demanded.

They came in time and again, surprisingly courageous, Joe had to admit, and time and again he decimated them. One by one, coolly, seldom wasting a shot. Not that he had to watch his ammunition, he had the squad's full supply. He estimated that before it was through he had inflicted approximately thirty casualties. Hits in the head, in the torso, the arms, legs. He had inflicted enough casualties to fill a field hospital. And it had all ended, finally, when a senior officer below had arrived on the scene, took in the irritating situation, and sent a dozen noncoms and junior officers, experienced men, to dig Joe out. Joe had remained only long enough for a few final shots, none of them effective, at long range, and had then hauled out and followed after his squad. He might possibly have got two or three more of his opponents, but only at his own risk. Besides, already the irritation and hate that he had built up while on the run, and while his squad mates were copping wounds, had left him and there was nausea in his belly at the slaughter he had perpetrated.

Or that time on the Louisiana Reservation in the fracas between Allied Petroleum and United Oil. Joe had been a lieutenant then and—

But he rejected this trend of thought and brought his attention back to Sam Soligen.

"Perhaps you're right," he admitted. "Some Low-Lower jerk, impressed by what he considers high pay and adventure, doesn't stand much of a chance against an old pro."

The gawky tee-ager broke into a toothy smile. "Gee, I wasn't arguing with you, major. I don't know anything about it. How about telling me about one of your fracases, eh? You know, some time you really got in the dill."

Joe snorted. He seldom met someone not of Category Military who didn't want a special detailed description of some gory action in which Joe had participated. And like all veterans of combat, there was nothing he liked less to do. Combat was something which, when done, you wished to leave behind you. Were brain washing really practicable, it was this you would wish to wash away.

But Joe, like others before him, down through the ages, had found a way out. He had a store of a dozen or so humorous episodes with which he could regale listeners. That time his horse's cinch had loosened when he was on a scouting mission and he had galloped around and around amidst a large company of enemy skirmishers, most of them running after him and trying to drag him from the horse's back, while he hung on for dear life.

But it occurred to him that the boy might better appreciate a tale which involved his father, the Telly reporter, and some act of daring the small man had performed the better to serve his fracas-buff audience.

He was well launched into the tale, boosting Freddy Soligen's part beyond reality, but not impossibly so, when that worthy entered the room, breaking it off.

While Freddy was shaking hands with his visitor, Sam said, "Hey, Papa, you never told me about that time you were surrounded by all the field artillery, and only you and Major Mauser and three other men got out."

Freddy grinned fondly at the boy and then looked his reproach at Joe. "What're you trying to do, make the life of a Telly reporter sound romantic to the kid? Stick to the priesthood, son, there's more chicken dinners involved." He saw Joe was impatient to talk to him. "How about leaving us alone for a while, Sam? We've got some business."

"Sure, Papa. I've got to memorize some Greek chants, anyway. How come they don't have all these rituals and all in some language everybody can understand?"

"Then everybody might understand them," Freddy said sourly. "Then what'd happen?"

His son said, "Major, maybe you can finish that story some other time, huh?"

Joe said, "Sure, sure, sure. It winds up with your father the hero and they bump him up to Upper-Upper and make him head of Category Communications."

"On the trank again," Freddy grumbled, but Joe sensed he wasn't particularly amused.

When the boy was gone, Joe Mauser told the Telly reporter of his interview with Stonewall Cogswell.

Freddy shook his head. "He wants you to fly that sailplane thing of yours again, huh? No. That won't do it. We need some gimmick, Joe. Something—"

Joe said impatiently, "You keep saying that. But, look, I'm a mercenary. A fighting man can't drop out of participation in the fracases if he expects the buffs to continue interest in him."

The little man tried to explain. "I'm not saying you're going to drop out of the fracases. But we need something where we can make you shine. Somewhere where you can be on every lens for a mile around."

Joe's face was still impatient.

Freddy said sourly, "Listen, you tried to handle all this by yourself, last time. You dreamed up that fancy glider gimmick and sold it to old Baron Haer. But did you do yourself any good with the buffs? Like Zen you did. All you did was louse up a perfectly promising fracas so far as they were concerned. Hardly a drop of blood was shed. Stonewall Cogswell just resigned when he saw what he was up against. Oh, sure, you won the battle for Vacuum Tube Transport, practically all by yourself, but that's not what the buff wants. He wants blood, he wants action, spectacular action. And you can't give it to him way up there in the air. Hey—!"

Joe looked at him, scowling questioningly.

Freddy said, slowly, "Why not?"

Joe Mauser growled, "What'd you mean, why not?"

Freddy said slowly, "Why can't you have some blood and guts combat, right up there in that glider?"

"Have you gone drivel-happy?"

But the little man was on his feet, pacing the floor quickly, irritably, but still happily. "A dogfight. A natural. Listen, you ever heard about dogfights, major?"

"You mean pitdogs, like in Wales, in the old days?"

"No, no. In the First War. All those early fighters. Baron Von Richthofen, the German, Albert Ball, the Englishman, René Fonck, the Frenchman. And all the rest. Werner Voss and Ernst Udet, and Rickenbacker and Luke Short."

Joe nodded at last. "I remember now. They'd have a Vickers or Spandau mounted so as to fire between the propeller blades. As I recall, that German, Richthofen, had some eighty victories to his credit."

"O.K. They called them dogfights. One aircraft against another. You're going to reintroduce the whole thing."

Joe was staring at him. Once again the Telly reporter sounded completely around the bend.

Freddy was impatiently patient. "We'll mount a gun on your sailplane and you'll attack those two gliders Cogswell says General McCord has."

Joe said, "The Sov-world observers would never stand still for it. In fact, there's a good chance that using gliders at all will be forbidden when the International Disarmament Commission convenes next month. If the Sov-world delegates vote against use of gliders as reconnaissance craft, the Neut-world will vote with them. Those Neut-world delegates vote against everything." Joe grunted. "It's true enough gliders were flown before the year 1900, but not the kind of advanced sailplanes you have to utilize for them to be practical. Certainly there were no gliders in use capable of carrying a machine gun."

Freddy demanded, "Look, what was the smallest machine gun in use in 1900?"

Joe considered. "Probably the little French Chaut-Chaut gun. It was portable by one man, the rounds were carried in a flat, circular pan. I think it goes back that far. They used them in the First War."

"Right! O.K., you had gliders. You had eight portable machine guns. All we're doing is combining them. It'll be spectacular. You'll be the most famous mercenary in Category Military and it'll be impossible for the Department not to bounce you to colonel and Low-Upper. Especially with me and every Telly reporter and fracas-buff magazine we've bribed yelling for it."

Joe's mouth manifested its tic, but he was shaking his head. "It wouldn't go, anyway. Suppose I caught one, or both, of those other gliders, busy at their reconnaissance and shot their tails off. So what? The fans still wouldn't have their blood and gore. We'd be so high they couldn't see the action. All they would be able to see would be the other glider falling."

Freddy stopped dramatically and pointed a finger at him in triumph. "That's where you're wrong. I'll be in the back seat of your sailplane with a portable camera. Get it! And every reporter on the ground will have the word, and his most powerful telescopic lens at the ready. Man, it'll be the most televized bit of fracas of this half of the century!"

CHAPTER EIGHT

When Major Joe Mauser entered the swank Agora Bar, the little afternoon dance band broke into a few bars of that tune which was beginning to pall on him.

"...I knew her heart was breaking, And to my heart in anguish pressed, The girl I left behind me."

Nadine looked up from the little table she occupied and caught the wry expression on his face and laughed.

"What price glory?" she said.

He took the chair across from her and chuckled ruefully. "All right," he said, "I surrender. However, if you think a theme song is bad, you'll be relieved at some of the other ideas my, ah, publicity agent had which I turned down."

She said, "Oh, did he want you to dash into some burning building and save some old lady's canary, or something?"

"Not exactly. However, he had a nightclub singer with a list of nine or ten victories behind her—"

"Victories?"

"Husbands. And I was to be seen escorting the singer around the nightclub circuit."

"A fate worse than death? But, truly, why did you turn him down?"

"I wanted to spend the time with you."

She made a moue. "So as to carry on our never-ending argument over the value of status?"

"No."

Her eyes dropped and there was a slight frown on her forehead. Joe interpreted it to mean that she took exception to one of Mid-Middle caste speaking to her in this wise. He said, flatly, "At least the tune is somewhat applicable tonight."

She looked up quickly, having immediately caught the meaning of his words. "Oh, Joe, you haven't taken another commission?"

"Why not? I'm a mercenary by trade, Nadine." He was vaguely irritated by her tone.

"But you admittedly made a small fortune on the last fracas. You were one of the very few investors in the whole country who expected Vacuum Tube Transport to boom, rather than go bankrupt. You simply don't *need* to risk your life further, Joe!"

He didn't bother to tell her that already the greater part of his small fortune had been siphoned off in Freddy Soligen's campaign to make him a celebrity. He said, instead, "The stock shares I'll make aren't particularly important, Nadine. But Stonewall Cogswell has pledged that if I'll fly for him in the Carbonaceous Fuel-United Miners fracas, he'll press my ambitions for promotion."

She said, her voice low, "Promotion in rank, or caste, Joe?"

"You know the answer to that."

"But, Joe, to risk your life, your *life*, Joe, for such a silly thing—"

He said softly, "Such a silly thing as attaining to a position which will enable me to court openly the girl I love?"

She flushed, looked into his face quickly. Her flush deepened and her eyes went to her folded hands, on the table.

He said nothing.

Nadine said finally, her voice so low as almost not to be heard, "Perhaps I would be willing to marry a man of Middle caste."

He was taken with surprise, but even in thrilling to the meaning of her words, his head was shaking in negation. "Nadine Haer, Category Medicine, Rank Doctor, Mid-Upper, married to Major Joseph Mauser, Category Military, Mid-Middle. Don't be ridiculous, Nadine. It would be as though back in the Twentieth Century you would have married a Negro or Oriental."

She was stirred with anger. "There is no law preventing marriage between castes!"

"Nor was there law, in most States, against marrying between races. But there were few who dared, and, of those, few who were allowed to be happy. It's no go, Nadine. Remember in the Exclusive Room the other night when the waiter questioned my presence in an Upper establishment and you had to tell him I was your guest? I don't desire to be your guest the rest of my life, Nadine."

The anger welled higher in her. "And do you think that in the remote case you do jump your caste to Upper, that I would marry you and then realize the rest of my life that our marriage was only possible due to your participation in mass slaughter for the sake of the slobbering multitudes of Telly fans?"

Joe said, "I wasn't going to bring the matter up until I had made Low-Upper caste."

"Well, sir, the matter is up. And I reject you in advance. Oh, Joe, if you have to persist in this status-hungry ambition of yours, drop the Category Military and get into something else. You have enough of a fortune to branch into various fields where your abilities would lead to advancement."

Again he didn't tell her that his fortune was all but dissipated. Instead, he said bitterly, "Those who have, get. The rich get richer, the poor get poorer. Things are rigged, these days, so that it's impossible to work your way to the top except in Military and Religion. The Uppers take care of their own, and at the same time make every effort to keep us of the lower orders from joining their sacred circle. I might make it in the Military, Nadine, but my chances in another field are so remote as to be laughable."

She stood and looked down at him emptily. "No," she said, "don't get up. I'm leaving, Major Mauser." He began to rise, to protest, but she said, her voice curt, "I have seen only one fracas on Telly in my entire life, and was so repelled that I vowed never to watch again. However, I am going to make an exception. I am going to follow this one, and if, as a result of your actions, even a single person meets death, I wish never to see you again. Do I make myself completely clear, Major Mauser?"

CHAPTER NINE

Marshal Stonewall Cogswell looked impudently around at this staff officers gathered about the chart table. "Gentlemen," he said, "I assume you are all familiar with the battle of Chancellorsville?"

No one bothered to answer and he chuckled. "I know what you are thinking, that had any of you refrained from a thorough study of the campaigns of Lee and Jackson, he would not be a member of my staff."

The craggy marshal traced with his finger on the great military chart before them. "Then you will have noticed the similarity of today's dispensation of forces to that of Joseph Hooker's Army of the Potomac and Lee's Army of Northern Virginia, on May 2, 1863." He pointed with his baton. "Our stream, here, would be the Rappahannock, this woods, the Wilderness. Here would be Fredericksburg and here Chancellorsville."

One of his colonels nodded. "My regiment occupies a position similar to that of Jubal Early."

"Absolutely correct," the marshal said crisply. "Gentlemen, I repeat, our troop dispensations, those of Lieutenant General McCord and myself, are practically identical. Now then, if McCord continues to move his forces here, across our modern day Rappahannock, he makes the initial mistake that finally led to the opening which allowed Jackson's brilliant fifteen-mile flanking march. Any questions, thus far?"

There were some murmurs, no questions. The accumulated years of military service of this group of veterans would have totaled into the hundreds.

"Very interesting, eh?" the marshal pursued. "Jed, your artillery is massed here. It's a shame that General Jack Altshuler has taken a commission with Carbonaceous Fuel. We could use his cavalry. He would be our J.E.B. Stuart, eh?"

Lieutenant Colonel Paul Warren cleared his throat unhappily. "Sir, Jack Altshuler is the best cavalryman in North America."

"I would be the last to deny it, Paul."

"Yes, sir. And he's fought half his fracases under you, sir."

"Your point, Paul?" the marshal said crisply.

"He knows your methods, sir. For that matter, so does Lieutenant General McCord. He's fought you enough."

There was silence in the staff headquarters, broken suddenly by Cogswell's curt chuckle. "Paul, I'm going to recommend to the Category Military Department, your promotion to full colonel on the strength of that. You were the first to see what I have been getting to. Gentlemen, do you realize what General McCord and his staff are doing this very moment? I would wager my reputation that they are poring over a campaign chart of the battle of Chancellorsville."

The craggy veteran bent back over the map again, his voice dropped all humor and he stabbed with his baton. "Here, here, and here. They expect us to duplicate the movements of Lee. Very good, we shall. But the advances of Lee and Jackson, we will make feints. And the feints made by Lee and Jackson will be our attacks in force. Gentlemen, we are going to literally reverse the battle of Chancellorsville. Major Mauser!"

Joe Mauser had been in the background as befitted his junior rank. Now he stepped to the table's edge. "Yes, sir."

The marshal indicated a defile. "Were we actually duplicating the Civil War battle, this would have been the right flank of Sedgwick's two army corps. We're not dealing in army corps these days but only regiments, however, the position is relatively as important. Jack Altshuler's cavalry is largely concentrated here. When the action is joined, he can move in one of three ways. Through this defile, is least likely. However, if his heavy cavalry *does* work its way through here, I must know immediately. This is crucial, Joe. Any questions?"

"No, sir."

The marshal turned his attention to his chief of artillery. "Jed, when we need your guns, we're going to need them badly, but I doubt if that time will develop until the second or third day of the fracas. Going to want as clever a job of camouflage done as possible."

The other scowled. "Camouflage, sir?"

"Confound it, yes. French term, I believe. Going to want your guns so hidden that those two gliders of McCord's will fail to spot them." The marshal grimaced in the direction of Joe Mauser, who, having his instructions, had fallen back from the table again. "When you reintroduced aerial observation to the fracas, major, you set off a whole train of related factors. Camouflage is going to be in every field officer's lexicon from this day on. Which reminds me." He looked to his artilleryman.

"Yes, sir."

"Put your mind to work on devising Maxim gun mounts to be used to keep enemy gliders at as high altitude as possible, or preferably, of course, to bring them down. We'll need an antiaircraft squadron, in short. Better put young Wiley on it."

"Yes, sir."

CHAPTER TEN

The airport nearest to the Grant Memorial Military Reservation was some ten miles distance from the borders which, upon the scheduling of a fracas, were closed to all aircraft, and to all persons unconnected with the fracas, with the exception only of Telly crews and military observers from the Sov-world and the Neut-world, present to satisfy themselves that weapons of the post-1900 era were not being utilized.

The distance, however, wasn't of particular importance. The powered aircraft which would tow Joe Mauser's glider to a suitable altitude preliminary to his riding the air currents, as a bird rides them, could also haul him to a point just short of the military reservation's border.

Joe Mauser turned up on the opening day of the fracas, which was scheduled for a period of one week, or less, if one or the other of the combatants was able to achieve total victory in such short order. He was accompanied by Freddy Soligen, who, for once, was without a crew to help him with his cameras and equipment. Instead, he sweated it out alone, helped only by Max Mainz who was being somewhat huffy about this Telly reporter taking over his position as observer.

They approached the sailplane, and while Joe Mauser checked it out, in careful detail, Freddy Soligen and Max began loading the equipment into the graceful craft's second seat, immediately behind the pilot. Max growled, "How in Zen you going to be able to lift all this weight, major, sir?"

Joe said absently, testing the ailerons, "We'll make it. Freddy isn't any heavier than you are, Max. Besides, this sailplane is a workhorse. I sacrificed gliding angle for weight carrying potential."

That meant absolutely nothing to Max Mainz, so he took it out by awarding the Telly reporter with a rare combination of glower and sneer.

Freddy said, "Oh, oh, here they come, Joe." However, he kept his head low, storing away his equipment, and seemingly ignored the approach of the three distinctive uniformed officers.

Joe said from the side of his mouth, "Get that you-know-what out of sight, soonest." He turned as the trio neared, came to attention and saluted.

The foremost of the three, his tunic so small at the waist that he could only have been wearing a girdle, answered the salute by tapping his swagger stick against the visor of his cap. "Major Mauser," he said in acknowledgment. He made no effort to shake hands, turning instead to his two companions. He said, "Lieutenant Colonel Krishnalal Majumdur, of Bombay, Major Mohamed Kamil, of Alexandria, may I introduce the…" There was all but a giggle in his tone. "…celebrated Major Joseph Mauser, who has possibly reintroduced aircraft to warfare."

Joe saluted and bowed in proper protocol. "Gentlemen, a pleasure." The two neutrals responded correctly, then stepped forward to shake his hand.

Colonel Lajos Arpid added, gently, "Or possibly he has not."

Joe looked at him. The Hungarian seemed to make a practice of turning up every time Joe Mauser was about to take off. The Sov-world representative said airily, "It will be up to the International Disarmament Commission to decide upon that when it convenes shortly, will it not?"

The Arab major was staring in fascination at the sailplane. He said to Joe, "Major Mauser, you are sure such craft were in existence before 1900? It would seem—"

Joe said definitely, "Designed as far back as Leonardo and flown in various countries in the Eighteenth Century." He looked at the Hungarian. "Including, so I understand, what was then Czarist Russia."

The Sov-world officer ignored the obvious needling, saying merely, "It is quite true that the glider was first flown by an obscure inventor in the Ukraine, however, that is not what particularly interests us today, major. Perhaps the commission will find that the use of the glider is permitted for observation, however, it is obvious that before the year 1900 by no stretch of the imagination could it be contended that they were, or could have been, used for, say, *bombing*." He turned quickly and pointed at Freddy Soligen, who, already seated in the sailplane, was watching them, his face not revealing his qualms. "What has that man been hiding within the craft?"

Joe said formally, "Gentlemen, may I introduce Frederic Soligen, Category Communications, Sub-division Telly News, Rank Senior Reporter. Mr. Soligen has been assigned to cover the fracas from the air."

Freddy looked at the Sov-world officer and said innocently, "Hiding? You mean my portable camera, and my power pack, and my auxiliary lenses, and my—"

"All right, all right," Arpád snapped. The Hungarian was no fool and obviously smelled something wrong in this atmosphere. He turned to Joe. "I would remind you, major, that you as an individual are responsible for any deviations from the basic Universal Disarmament Pact. You, and any of your superiors who can be proven to have had knowledge of such deviation."

"I am familiar with the articles of war, as detailed in the pact," Joe said dryly. "And now, gentlemen, I am afraid my duty calls me." He bowed stiffly, saluted correctly. "A pleasure to make your acquaintance Colonel Majumdur, Major Kamil. Colonel Arpád, a pleasure to renew acquaintance."

They answered his salute and stared after him as he climbed into the sailplane and signaled to the pilot of the lightplane which was to tow him into the air. Max Mainz ran to the tip of one wing, lifting it from the ground and steadying the glider until forward motion gave direction and buoyancy.

Freddy Soligen growled, "Zen! If they'd known I had a machine gun tucked away in this tripod case."

Joe said unhappily, "The Sovs have obviously decided to put up a howl about the use of aircraft in the West-world."

He shifted his hand on the stick, gently, and the glider which had been sliding along on its single wheel, lifted ever so gently into the air. Joe kept it at an altitude of about six feet until the lightplane was air-borne.

Freddy growled, "How come the Hungarians have become so important in the Sov-world? I thought it was the Russians who started their whole shooting-match."

Joe said wryly, "That's something some of the early timers like Stalin didn't figure out when they began moving in on their neighbors. They could have learned a lesson from Hollywood about the Hungarians. What was the old saying? *If you've got a Hungarian for a friend, you don't need any enemies.*"

Freddy laughed, even as he looked apprehensively over the sailplane's side. He said, "Yeah, or that other one. The Hungarians are the only people who can enter a revolving door behind you and come out in front."

Joe said, "Well, that's what happened to the Russians." He pointed. "There's the reservation. We'll be cutting from the airplane in a moment now. Listen, were you able to find out who either of General McCord's glider pilots are?"

"Yeah," Freddy told him. "Both are captains. One named Bob Flaubert and the other Jimmy Hideka."

"Bob Flaubert?" Jeb growled. "He's an artilleryman. We've been in the dill together half a dozen times." Freddy was staring below, trying to understand the terrain from this perspective. While Joe was tripping the lever which let the tow rope drop away from the glider, the Telly reporter said, "Both of them used to fly lightplanes for sport. When you started this new glider angle, they must've seen the possibilities and took it up immediately. But you oughta be able to fly circles around them, they just haven't had the time for experience with planes without motors."

"Bob, eh?" Joe said softly. "He saved my life once. Five minutes later, I saved his."

Freddy looked at him quickly. "Zen!" he complained. "It's no time to be thinking of that. So now you're even with him. And you're both hired mercenaries in a fracas."

"But I've got a gun and he hasn't," Joe growled.

"Good!" Freddy snapped at him.

They had cut away from the lightplane and Joe headed for the area which Cogswell had ordered him particularly to keep scanned. Jack Altshuler was a fox, in combat. His heavy cavalry had more than once swung a fracas.

At the same time, he kept himself alert for the other gliders. It seemed probable, since the enemy forces had two, that they would use them in relays. Which meant, in turn, that it was unlikely Joe would find them both in the air at once. In other words, if he attacked the one, possibly shooting it down, then the other would be warned, would mount a gun of its own, and it would no longer be a matter of shooting a clay pigeon.

Joe turned to mention this over his shoulder to Freddy Soligen, just in time to catch the shadow above and behind him.

"Holy Zen!" he snapped, kicking right rudder, thrusting his stick to the right and forward.

"What the devil!" Freddy protested, looking up from adjusting a lens on his camera.

Three or four thirty-caliber slugs tore holes in their left wing, the rest of the burst missing completely.

Joe dove sharply, gained speed, winged over and reached desperately for altitude. The other—no, the *others* were above him. He yelled back at the cameraman, "Put that Chaut-Chaut gun together for me. Be ready to hand me pans of ammo. And if you want blood and gore on that Tellylens of yours, get going!"

It still hadn't got through to the smaller man. "What in devil's going on?"

Joe banked again, grabbing for a current rising along a hill slope, circled, circled, reaching for altitude before they could get over to him and make another pass. He snapped bitterly, "Did I say something about poor old Bob Flaubert not having a gun, while I did? Well, poor old Bob's obviously got at least as much fire power as we have. Freddy, I'm afraid matters have pickled."

The other was startled.

"Do I have to draw a picture?" Joe said. "Look." He pointed to where the other two crafts circled, possibly a hundred meters above and five hundred to the right of them. The other two gliders bore a single passenger apiece, and were seemingly moving as quietly as were Joe and Freddy, but gliders in motion are deceptive. Joe shot a glance at his rate of climb indicator. He was doing all right at six meters per second, a thousand feet a minute, considering his weight.

Freddy had at last awakened to the fact that they were in combat and even that the enemy had drawn first blood. The wound taken in their wing was not serious, from Joe's viewpoint, but the torn holes in the fabric were obvious. But the little man had not gained his intrepid reputation as a Telly cameraman without cause. He moved fast, both to get the small French machine gun into Joe's hands and to get himself into action as a cameraman.

He snapped, "What's the situation?"

Joe, circling, circling, praying the updraft wouldn't give out on him before it did on the others, on their opposite hill, said, "We weigh too much. Altitude counts. What've you got back there that can be thrown out?" As he talked, he was shrugging himself out of his leather flying jacket.

"Nothing," Freddy said in anguish. "I cut down my equipment to the barest, like you said."

"You've got extra lenses and stuff, out with them." Joe tossed his coat over the glider's side, began unlacing his shoes. "And all your clothes. Clothes are heavy."

"I need my equipment to get long-range shots, like when one of them crashes!" The little man was scanning the others through his view-finder, even as he argued, and shrugging out of his own jacket.

The updraft gave out and the rate of climb meter began to register a drop. Joe swore and shot a glance at his opponents. Happily, they, too, had lost their currents, both were now heading for him.

Joe clipped out to his companion. "We're not going to be getting shots of them crashing, unless we lose more weight. Overboard with everything you can possibly afford, Freddy. That's an order."

There was one thing in his favor. He had a year's flying experience, more than six months of it in this very glider. The stick and rudderbar were as though appendages of his body. One flies by the seat of his pants, in a soaring glider, and Joe flew his as though born in it. The others, obviously, were as yet not thoroughly used to engineless craft.

He banked away from them, flying as judiciously as possible, begrudging each foot dropped. He could feel the craft jump lightly each time the cursing Telly reporter jettisoned another article of equipment, his pants, or his shoes.

The others evidently had their guns fix-mounted, to fire straight ahead. Joe wondered, even as he slid away from them, how they managed to escape detection from the Sov-world and Neut-world field observers. Well, that could be worried about later.

One of them fired at him at too great a range, and then both, realizing that they were dropping altitude too quickly and that soon Joe would be on their level, turned away and sought a new updraft. As they banked, their faces were clearly discernible. One raised a hand in mocking salute.

"Look at that curd-loving Bob," Joe laughed grudgingly. "Here, let me have that gun."

He steadied the small mitrailleuse on the edge of the cockpit, holding the craft's stick between his knees, and squeezed off a burst which rattled through the other's fuselage without apparent damage. The foe glider slid away quickly, losing precious altitude in the maneuver.

"Ah, ha," Joe said wolfishly. "So now they know we've got a stinger too."

"I got that," Freddy crowed. "I got it perfectly. Listen, we're too high for the boys down below. Get lower so they can get you on lens, Joe. The other Telly teams. Every fracas buff in North America is watching this."

Joe snorted his disgust. "I hope every fracas buff in North America chokes on his trank pills," he snarled. "We're in the dill, Freddy. Understand? We're too heavy, and there's two of them and one of us. On top of that, those are Maxim guns they've got mounted, not peashooters like this Chaut-Chaut."

"That's your side of it," Freddy said, not unhappily. "I take care of the photography. Get closer, Joe. Get closer."

Joe had found another light updraft and gained a few hundred feet, but so had the others. They circled, circled.

His experience balanced their advantage of the lesser weight. Happily, their glide ratios didn't seem to be any better than his own. Had they high performance gliders of forty, or even thirty-five, gliding angle ratios, he would have been lost.

"Nothing else you can toss out?" he growled at Freddy.

"What the Zen!" Freddy muttered nastily. "You want me to jump?"

"That's an idea," Joe growled wolfishly, even as he circled, circled. "I should have realized when you were giving me your fling about reintroducing aerial warfare, that it wasn't an idea that others couldn't have. It was just as easy for Bob to mount a gun as it was for us. Now we're both being kept from doing reconnaissance by the other and—"

Joe Mauser broke it off in mid-sentence and his face blanched. He shot a quick look downward. All three gliders had climbed considerably, and the terrain below was indistinct.

Joe snapped, "Hand me those glasses!"

"What glasses? What's the matter?" Freddy complained. "Try to get closer to them and let me get a close-up of you giving them a burst."

"My binoculars!" Joe snapped urgently. "I want to see what's going on below."

"Oh," Freddy said. "I threw them out. Along with all the rest of the equipment. Glasses, semaphore flags, that sun blinker you had. All of it went overboard with my extra lenses."

The craft was so banked as almost to have the wings perpendicular to earth. Joe shot an agonized look at the smaller man, then back again at the earth below, trying desperately to narrow his eyes for keener vision.

Freddy said, "What in Zen's the matter with you? What difference does it make what they're doing down below? We're all occupied up here, thanks."

"This is a frame-up," Joe growled. "Bob and that other pilot. They weren't out on reconnaissance, this morning. They were laying for me. They're out to keep me from seeing what's going on down there. And I know what's going on. Jack Altshuler's pulling a fast one. Here we go, Freddy, hang on!"

He slapped his flap brake lever with his left hand, winged over and began dropping like a shot as his gliding angle fell off from twenty-five to one to ten to one. In seconds the other two gliders were after him, riding his tail.

Freddy Soligen, his eyes bugging, shot a look of fear at the two trailing craft, both of which, periodically, showed brilliant cherries at their prows. Maxim guns, emitting their blessings.

The Telly reporter turned desperately back to Joe Mauser, pounding him on the shoulder. His physical fear was secondary to another. "Joe! You're on lens with every Telly team down there, and you're running!"

"Cut that out," Joe rapped. "Duck your head. Let me train this gun over you. I've got to keep those jokers from shooting off our tail before I can get to the marshal."

"The marshal!" Freddy yelled. "You can't get to him anyway. I told you I threw away your semaphore flags, your blinker—everything. This country's hilly. You can't get your message to him anyway. Listen, Joe, you've still got time. You can stunt these things better than those two can."

"Duck!" Joe snarled. He let loose a burst at the pursuing gliders over the smaller man's head, and just missing his own tail section.

They sped down almost to tree level at fantastic speed for a glider. The two enemy craft were hot after them, their guns *flac, flac, flacing* in continuous excitement, trying to catch Joe in sights, as he kicked rudder, right, left, right, in evasive maneuver.

He guess had been correct. The swashbuckling Jack Altshuler had know his many times commander even better than Cogswell had realized. Instead of three alternative maneuvers open to the wily cavalryman, he'd ferreted out a fourth and his full force, hauling mountain guns on mule back with them, were trailing over a supposedly impossible mountain path which originally could not have been more then a deer track.

Freddy Soligen, in back, was holding his head in his hands in surrender. He could have focused on the troops below, but the desire wasn't in him. Not one fracas buff in a hundred could comprehend the complications of combat, the need for adequate reconnaissance—the need for Joe to get through.

He made one last plea. "Joe, we've put everything into this. Every share of stock you've accumulated. All I have, too. Don't you realize what you're doing, so far as the buffs are concerned? Those two half-trained pilots behind have you on the run."

Joe growled, "And twenty thousands lads down below are depending on me to report on Altshuler's horse."

"But you can't win, anyway. You can't get your message to Cogswell!"

Joe shot him a wolfish grin. "Wanta bet? Ever heard of a crash landing, Freddy? Hang on!"

CHAPTER ELEVEN

Stretched out on the convalescent bed in the Category Military rest home, Joe grinned up at his visitor and said ruefully, "I'd salute, sir, but my arms seem to be out of commission. And, come to think of it, I'm out of uniform."

Cogswell looked down at him, unamused. "You've heard the news?"

Joe caught the other's tone and his face straightened. "You mean the Disarmament Commission?"

Cogswell said brittlely, "They found against the use of aircraft, other than free balloons, in any military action. They threw the book, Mauser. The court ruled that you, Robert Flaubert and James Hideka be stripped of rank and forbidden the Category Military. You have also been fined all stock shares in your possession other than those unalienably yours as a West-world citizen."

Joe's face went empty. It was only then that he realized that the other was attired in the uniform of a brigadier general. The direction of his eyes was obvious.

Cogswell shrugged bitterly. "My Upper caste status helped me. I could pull just enough strings that the Category Military Department, in conjunction with the rulings of the International Disarmament Commission merely reduced me in rank and belted me with a stiff fine. Your friend—your former friend, I should say, Freddy Soligen, testified in my behalf. Testified that I had no knowledge of your mounting a gun."

The former marshal cleared his throat. "His testimony was correct. I had no such knowledge and would have issued orders against it, had I known. The fact that you enabled me to rescue the situation into which I'd been sucked, helps somewhat my feelings toward you, Mauser. But only somewhat."

Joe could imagine the other's bitterness. He had fought his way up the hard way to that marshal's baton. At his age, he wasn't going to regain it.

Brigadier general Stonewall Cogswell hesitated for a moment, then said, "One other thing. United Miners has repudiated your actions even to the point of refusing the cost of your hospitalization. I told the Category Medicine authorities to put your bill on my account."

Joe said quite stiffly, "That won't be necessary, sir."

"I'm afraid you'll find it is, Mauser." The former marshal allowed himself a grimace. "Besides, I owe you something for that spectacular scene when you came skimming over the treetops, the two enemy gliders right behind you, then stalling your craft and crashing into that tree not thirty feet from my open air headquarters. Admittedly, in forty years of fracases, I've never seen anything so confoundedly dramatic."

"Thank you, sir."

The old soldier grunted, turned and marched from the room.

CHAPTER TWELVE

Freddy Soligen had been miraculously saved from the physical beating taken by Joe Mauser in the crash. The pilot, sitting so close before him, cushioned with his own body that of the Telly reporter.

For that matter, he had been saved the financial disaster as well, save for that amount he had contributed to the campaign to increase Mauser's stature in the eyes of the buffs. His Category Communications superiors had not even charged him for the cost of the equipment he had jettisoned from the glider during the flight, nor that which had been destroyed in the crash. If anything, his reputation with his higher-ups was probably better than ever. He'd been in there pitching, as a Telly reporter, right up until the end when the situation had completely pickled.

All that he had lost was his dream. It had been so close to the grasping. He could almost have tasted the sweetness of victory. Joe Mauser, at the ultimate top of the hero-heap. Joe Mauser accepting bounces in both rank and caste. And then, Joe Mauser being properly thankful and helpful to

Freddy and Sam Soligen, in their turn. So near the realization of the dream.

He entered his house wearily, finally free of all the ridiculous questioning of the commission and the courts martial of Mauser and Cogswell, and Flaubert, Hideka and their commander, General McCord. All had been found guilty, though in different degrees. Using weapons of warfare which post-dated 1900. Than which there was no greater crime between nations.

He tossed the brief case he had carried to a table, and made his way to the living room, heading for the auto-bar and some straight spirits.

A voice said, "Hi, Papa."

He looked up, not immediately recognizing the Category Military, Rank Private, before him.

Then he said weakly, "Sam!" His legs gave way, and he sat down abruptly on the couch which faced the wall which was the Telly screen.

The boy said, awkwardly, "Surprise, Papa!"

His father said, very slowly, "What...in...Zen...are... you...doing...in...that...outfit?"

Sam grinned ruefully, albeit proudly. "Aw, it would've taken a century for me to make full priest, Papa. The only way to do is like Major Mauser. You didn't know this, but, I've been following the fracases all along. Especially when you were the reporter. I've watched every fracas you've covered for years. I guess you know I'm pretty proud of you."

"Sam! What are you doing in that uniform! Answer me!"

The boy flushed. "I'm old enough, Papa. I switched categories. I've signed up with Chrysler-Ford in their fracas with Hovercar Sports. They're taking me on as infantryman."

"Infantryman?" Freddy winced, and closed his eyes. "Listen, boy, where'd you get the idea that—" He started over again. "But all your life I've given you the inside on the Category Military, Sam. All your life. No trank in our home. No watching the Telly day in and out. You've gone to *school*. More than I ever did. You were going to be a Temple priest—"

Sam sat down too, vaguely surprised at this father's reaction. "Aw, Papa, everybody's a fracas buff now. Everybody. You can't get away from it. I…well, I want to be like Major Mauser. Get so all the fans know me, want my autograph, all that. And all the excitement of being in a fracas, getting in the dill, and all. I just want to be like the other fellas, Papa."

Freddy could only stare at him.

Sam tried to explain. "Shucks, it was really you that made me want to become a mercenary. You're the best Telly reporter of them all. When *you* cover a fracas, Papa, you really do it. You can see *everything*." He shook his head in admiration. "Gosh, you really feel the emotion. It's the most exciting thing in the world."

"Yeah, son," Freddy Soligen said emptily. "I suppose it is."

CHAPTER THIRTEEN

Joe was able to get around on auto-crutches by the time she finally arrived—a stereotype visitor. Done up brightly, a box of candy in one hand, flowers in the other. He could see her coming across the lawn, from the visitor's offices. He wished that he had worn his other suit. His clothing was on the skimpy side when uniforms were subtracted.

She came up to him. "Well, Joe."

He looked at the flowers and attempted a grin. "Lilies would have been more appropriate, considering the shape I'm in."

Nadine said, "I've just been talking to the staff doctors. You're not in as bad shape as all that. Some bone mending, is all."

The grin turned wry. "I wasn't just thinking of the physical shape." He settled to the stone bench which stood to one side of the walk he had been exercising upon before her arrival. For a moment, she remained standing.

He looked up at her. "Well," he said. "I didn't break your condition," he said. "Am I still receivable?"

She frowned.

Joe said, bitterly, "You told me that you were going to take the fracas in and if my actions resulted in any casualties, you never wanted to see me again."

She took the place beside him. "I did watch. For a time, the rest of the battle going on below was ignored and you were full on lens for at least twenty minutes. I was never so frightened in my life."

Joe said, "The first step toward becoming a buff. First you're scared. Vicariously. But it's fun to become scared, when nothing can really happen to you. It becomes increasingly exciting to see others threatened with death— and then actually to die before you. After a while, you're hooked."

She looked carefully at the flowers. "That's not exactly what I meant. I was frightened for you, Joe. Not thrilled."

He looked at her for a long moment. Finally he breathed deeply and said, "Well, you'll never have to go through that again. I'm no longer in the Category Military, I suppose you know."

"It was on the news, Joe." She laughed without amusement. "In fact, I knew even before. Balt was tried, too."

"Balt? Your brother?"

She nodded. "You first used your glider in that fracas for father and Vacuum Tube Transport. Now that the commission has ruled against gliders, Balt, now head of the family, has been both fined and expelled from Category Military for life. It hasn't exactly improved his liking for you."

Joe hadn't heard of it, however, he had little sympathy for Balt Haer, nor interest in him. He said, "Why did you take so long to come?"

"I was thinking, Joe."

"And then you finally came."

"Yes."

He looked away and into unseen distances. Finally he cleared his throat and said, "Nadine, the first time I ever talked to you to any extent, I mentioned that I wanted to achieve the top in this status world of ours. I mentioned that I hadn't built this world, and possibly didn't even approve of it, but since I'm in it and have no other recourse, I must follow its rules."

She nodded. "I remember. And I said, why not try and change the rules?"

Joe nodded. He moistened his lips carefully. "O.K. Now I'm willing to listen. How do we go about changing the rules?"

CHAPTER FOURTEEN

Dr. Nadine Haer, Category Medicine, Mid-Upper caste, was driving and with considerable enjoyment resultant not only from her destination, long desired, now to be realized, but also from the sheer exuberance of handling the vehicle. Since pre-history, man's pleasure in the physical control of a speedy vehicle has been superlative, particularly when that vehicle is known by the driver to be unique in its class. The

Hittite charioteer, bowling across the landscape of Anatolia, a Sterling Moss carefully tooling his automobile around the multi-curves of the Upper Cornice on the Riviera, or a Nadine Haer delicately trimming the controls of a sports model Hovercar.

She shot a quick glance at Joe Mauser, formerly of Category Military, formerly Rank Major, now an unemployed Mid-Middle who slouched in the bucketseat next to her. He noticed neither speed nor direction.

Nadine called, above the wind, "Zen, Joe! Where did you ever acquire such a car? It must have been built entirely by hand, and by Swiss watchmakers."

Joe stirred and shrugged. Newly from the hospital, he was still deep in the gloom of his recent loss of the dream, the defeat of his life-long ambitions. He said, "A buff gave it to me."

She slowed down, the better to frown at him in amazement. "*Gave* it to you? Why the thing is priceless."

Joe sighed and told her the salient details. "Quite a few mercenaries manage to acquire a private fracas-buff." He defined the term for her. "He makes a hobby of your career. Winds up knowing more about it than you, yourself can possibly remember. He follows every fracas you get into. Knows every time you cop one, how serious it was, how long you were in hospital. He glories each time you get a promotion, is in gloom each time your side loses a fracas. He's got pictures of you in various poses taken from the fracas-buff magazines, and files away all articles in which your name appears."

"Zen!" Nadine laughed in deprecation.

"That's just the beginning. After a while he starts writing you fan letters, wanting autographed portraits, wanting a souvenir—sometimes nothing more exciting than a button off your uniform. More often they want a gun, sword or combat knife, particularly one they saw you using in some fracas or other. They usually offer to pay for such, sometimes quite fabulous amounts. Other times they want a bit of bloody uniform, your own true blood from a time when you were in the dill and managed to cop one."

Nadine was astonished. Antagonistic as she was, herself, to the fracases, she wasn't particularly knowledgeable about all their ramifications. She said, repelled, "But doesn't such morbidity disgust you? This fawning, this slobbering—"

Joe grunted. "All part of the game. A mercenary without buffs to boost him, to form fracas-buff clubs and such, hasn't much chance of promotion. So far as disgust is concerned, you'd have to see one of the really far-out ones. The gleam in an ordinarily fishlike eye when he recounts the time you killed three men in hand-to-hand combat, equipped only with an entrenching tool, when they came at you with bayonets. The trace of spittle, running down from the side of his mouth."

"And this buff of yours. Why did he give you this perfectly marvelous car?"

"It was a she, not a he," Joe said.

Nadine's voice changed infinitesimally. "You mean you accepted a gift of this value from a...woman?"

Joe looked at her and grinned sourly. "I wasn't in much of a position to refuse. The gift was in her will. She was well into her nineties when she died. She was an Upper-Upper, by the way, and the most knowledgeable fracas buff I ever met. She knew the intimate details of every fracas since Tiglath-Pileser and his Assyrians captured Babylon. She could argue for an hour on whether Parmenion or Alexander the Great should have been given the credit for the victory over the Persians at Issus." Joe grunted. "I suppose there should be a moral somewhere about this kindly old lady who was the outstanding fracas buff of them all."

Nadine Haer was in the process of hitting the drop lever with her left hand as they slowed and headed for the entrance to a parking area. She said brittlely, "The moral is that you can have slobs at any level in society. Being an Upper doesn't guarantee anything."

Joe sighed, "Here we go again." He looked about him, scowling. "Which brings to mind. Where *are* we going? These are governmental buildings, aren't they?"

They were sinking quickly, below street level, now in the power of the auto-parker. Nadine turned off the engine and released the controls. She said, cryptogrammicly, "We are going to see about doing something with your abilities other than shooting at people, or being shot at."

When the car was parked, she led the way to an elevator. Joe said wryly, "Oh, great. I love mysteries. When do we find out who killed the victim?"

Nadine looked at him from the side of her eyes. "I killed the victim," she said. "Major Mauser, mercenary by trade, is now no more."

There was bitterness in him and he found no ability to respond to what was meant as humor in her words. He followed her silently and his puzzlement grew with him. The office building through which they moved was as well done as any he could ever remember having observed, even on the Telly. Surely they couldn't be in the Octagon or the New White House. But, if so, why?

Nadine said. "Here we are," and indicated a door which opened at their approach.

There was a receptionist in the small office beyond, a bit of ostentation Joe Mauser seldom met with in the modern world. What in the name of Zen could anyone need with other than an auto-receptionist? Didn't efficiency mean anything here?

The receptionist said, "Good afternoon, Dr. Haer. Mr. Holland is expecting you."

It came to Joe now—Philip Holland, secretary to Harlow Mannerheim, the Minister of Foreign Affairs. He had met the man a few months ago at Nadine's home in that swank section of Greater Washington once known as Baltimore. But he had no idea what Nadine had in mind bringing him here. Evidently, she was well enough into the graces of the bureaucrat to barge into his office during working hours. Surprising in itself, since, although she was an Upper born, still governmental servants can't be at the beck of every hereditary aristocrat in the land.

Holland stood up briefly at their entrance and shook hands quickly, almost abruptly, held a chair for Nadine, motioned to another one for Joe. He sat down again and said into an inter-office telly-mike, "Miss Mikhail, the dossier on Joesph Mauser, and would you request Frank Hodgson to drop in?"

What was obviously the dossier slid from the desk chute and Holland leafed through it, as though disinterested. He said, "Joseph Mauser, born Mid-Lower, Clothing Category, Sub-division Shoes, Branch Repair." Holland looked up. "A somewhat plebian beginning, let us admit."

A tic manifested itself at the side of Joe Mauser's mouth, but he said nothing. If long years of the military had taught him anything, it was patience. The other man had the initiative now, let him use it.

Holland cast his eyes ceilingward, and, without referring to the dossier before him, said, "Crossed categories at the age of seventeen to Military, remaining a Rank Private for three years at which time promoted to corporal. Sergeant followed in another three years and upon reaching the rank of lieutenant, at the age of twenty-five was bounced in caste to High-Lower. After distinguishing himself in a fracas between Douglas-Boeing and Lockheed-Cessna was further raised to Low-Middle caste. By the age of thirty had reached Mid-Middle caste and Rank Captain. By thirty-three, the present, had been promoted to major, and had been under consideration for Upper-Middle caste."

That last, Joe had not know about, however, he said now, "Also at present, expelled from participation in future fracases on any level of rank, and fined his complete resources beyond the basic common stock issued him as a Mid-Middle." His voice was bitter.

Philip Holland said briskly, "The risks run by the ambitious."

The office door opened and a tall stranger entered. He had a strange gait, one shoulder held considerably lower than the other, to the point that Joe would have thought it the result of a wound hadn't the other obviously never been a soldier. The newcomer, office pallor heavily upon him, but his air of languor obviously assumed and artificial, darted his eyes around the room, to Holland, Nadine, and then to Joe where they rested for a moment.

He murmured some banality to Nadine, indicative of a long acquaintance and then approached Joe, who had automatically come to his feet, and extended a hand to be shaken. "I'm Frank Hodgson. You're Joe Mauser. I'm not fracas buff, but I know enough about current developments to know that. Welcome aboard, Joe."

Joe shook the hand offered, in some surprise.

"Welcome aboard?" he said.

Hodgson looked to Philip Holland, his eyebrows raised in question.

Holland said crisply, "You're premature, Frank. Dr. Haer and Mauser have just arrived."

"Oh." The newcomer found himself a chair, crossed his legs and fumbled in his pocket for a pipe, leaving it to the others to resume the conversation he had interrupted.

Philip Holland said to Joe, "Frank is assistant to Wallace Pepper." He looked at Hodgson and frowned. "I don't believe you have any other title do you, Frank?"

"I don't think so," Frank yawned. "Can't think of any."

Joe Mauser looked from one to the other, confusion adding to confusion within him. Wallace Pepper was the long time head of the North American Bureau of Investigation, having held that position under at least four administrations.

Nadine said dryly, "Which goes to show you, Joe, just how much titles mean. Commissioner Pepper has been all but senile for the past five years. Frank, here, is the true head of the bureau."

Frank Hodgson said mildly, "Why, Nadine, that's a rather strong statement."

Joe blurted, "Head of the Bureau of Investigation! I had gathered the impression I was being taken to meet some members of an underground, organized for the purpose of, as it was put, changing the present rules of government."

Frank Hodgson grinned at Nadine and laughed softly, "That's a gentle way of describing revolution."

Holland looked at Joe Mauser and said briskly, "I'll try to take you off the hook as quickly as possible, Joe. Tell me, when you hear the word revolution, what comes first to your mind?"

Joe, flustered, said, "Why, I don't know. Fighting, riots, people running around in the streets with banners. That sort of thing."

"Um-m-m," Holland nodded, "The common conception. However, a social revolution isn't, by definition, necessarily bloody. Picture a gigantic wheel, Joe. We'll call it the wheel of history. From time to time it makes a turn, forward, we hope, but sometimes backward. Such a turn is a revolution. Whether or not there is anybody under the wheel at the time of turning, is beside the point. The revolution takes place whether or not there is bloodshed."

He thought a moment. "Or you might compare it to childbirth. The fact that there is pain in childbirth, or, if through modern medical science, the pain is eliminated, is beside the point. Childbirth consists of a new baby coming into the world. The mother might even die, but childbirth has taken place. She might feel no pain whatsoever, under anesthetic, but childbirth has taken place."

Joe said carefully, "I'm no authority, but it seems to me that usually if changes take place in a socio-economic system without bloodshed, we call it evolution. Revolution is when they take place with conflict."

Holland shook his head. "No. Poor definitions. Among other things, don't confuse revolts, civil wars, and such with revolution. They aren't the same thing. You can have civil war, military revolts and various civil disturbances without having a socio-economic revolution. Let's use this for an example. Take a fertile egg. Inside of it a chick is slowly developing, slowly evolving. But it is still an egg. The chick finally grows tiny wings, a beak, even little feathers. Fine. But so far it's just evolution, within the shell of the egg. But one day that chick cannot develop further without breaking the shell and freeing itself of what was once its factor of defense but now threatens its very life. The shell must go. When that culminating action takes place, you have a revolutionary change and we are no longer dealing with an egg, but a chicken."

Joe, one by one, looked at the three of them. He said, finally, to Nadine, rather than to the men, "What's this got to do with me?"

She leaned forward in her earnestness. "All your life you've revolted against the *status quo*, Joe. You've beaten your head against the situation that confronted you, against a society you felt didn't allow you to develop your potentialities. But now you admit you've been wrong. What is needed is to..." She shot a defiant glance at Frank Hodgson, to his amusement. "...change the rules if the race is to get back onto the road to progress." She shrugged. "Very well. You can't expect it to be done single handed. You need an organization. Others who feel the same way you do. Here we are."

He was truly amazed now. When he had finally admitted interest in what Nadine had hinted to be a subversive organization, he'd had in mind some secretive group, possibly making their headquarters in a hidden cellar, complete with primitive printing press, and possibly some weapons. He most certainly hadn't expected to be introduced to the secretary of the Foreign Minister, and the working head of the North American Bureau of Investigation.

Joe blurted, "But...but you mean you Uppers are actually planning to subvert your own government?"

Holland said, "I'm not an Upper. I'm a Mid-Middle. What're you Frank?"

"Darned if I know," Hodgson said. "I forget. I think I was bounced up to Upper-Middle about ten years ago, for some reason or other, but I was busy at the time and didn't pay much attention. Every once in a while one of the Uppers I work with gets all excited about it and wants to jump me to Upper, but somehow or other we've never got around to it. What difference does it make?"

Joe Mauser was not the type to let his mouth fall agape, but he stared at the other, unbelievingly.

"What's the matter?" Hodgson said.

"Nothing," Joe said.

Philip Holland said briskly, "Let's get on with it. Nadine..." His voice had a dry quality. "...is one of our most efficient talent scouts. It was no mistake I met you at her home, a few weeks back, Joe. She thought you were potentially one of us. I admit to having formed the same opinion, upon our brief meeting. I now put the question to you direct. Do you wish to join our organization, the purpose of which is admittedly, to change our present socio-economic system and, as Nadine put it, get back on the road to progress?"

"Yes," Joe said. "I do."

"Very well, welcome aboard, as Frank said. Your first assignment will take you to Budapest."

They were throwing these curves too fast for Joe. Noted among his senior officers as a quick man, thinking on his feet, he still wasn't up to this sort of thing. "Budapest!" he ejaculated. "The capital of the Sov-world? But...but *why*—?"

Philip Holland looked at him patiently. "There are many ramifications to revolution, Joe. Particularly in this present day with its Frigid Fracas which has gone on for generations between the West-world and the Sov-world and with the Neut-world standing at the sidelines glaring at us both. You see, really efficient revolutions may simply not look like revolutions at all—just unusual results of historic accidents. And if we're going to make this one peacefully, we've got to take every measure to assure efficiency. One of these measures involves a thorough knowledge of where the Sov-world stands, and what it might do if there were any signs of a changing in the *status quo* here in the West-world."

Frank Hodgson said idly, "I believe you have met Colonel Lajos Arpád."

Joe said, puzzled still again, "Why, yes. One of their military attachés. An observer of our fracases to see whether or not the Universal Disarmament Pact is violated."

"But also, Colonel Arpád is probably the most competent espionage agent working out of Budapest."

"That corseted, giggling nincompoop!"

Frank Hodgson laughed softly. "If even an old pro like yourself hasn't spotted him, then we have one more indication of Arpád's abilities."

Philip Holland took up the ball again. "The presence of Colonel Arpád in Greater Washington is no coincidence. He is here for something, we're not sure what. However, rumors have been coming out of the Sov-world, and particularly Siberia, and the more backward countries to the south, such as Sinkiang. Rumors of an underground organized to overthrow the Sovs."

"And that religious thing," Nadine added.

Frank Hodgson murmured, "Yes, indeed. We received two more reports of it today."

All looked at him. He said to Joe, "Some fanatic in Siberia. A Tuvinian, one of the Turkic-speaking peoples in that area once called Tannu-Tuva, and now the Tuvinian Autonomous Oblast. He's attracting quite a following. Destroy the machines. Go back to the old way. Till the soil by hand. Let the women spin and weave, make clothing on the hand loom once more. Ride horses, rather than hovercraft and jets. That sort of thing. And, oh yes, kill those who stand in the way of this holy mission."

"And you mean this is catching hold in this day and age?" Joe said.

"Like wildfire," Hodges said easily. "And I wouldn't be too very surprised if it would do the same over here.

Pressures are generating, in this world of ours. We'll either make changes peaceably or Zen knows what will happen. The Sovs haven't been exposed to religion for several generations, Joe. Probably the Party heads had forgotten it as a potential danger. Here in the West-world we do better. The Temple provides us with a pressure valve in that particular area, but I still wouldn't like to see our trank and Telly bemused morons subjected to a sudden blast of revival-type religion."

Joe looked back at Holland. "I still don't get my going to Budapest. How, why, when?"

Holland glanced at a desk watch and became brisk. "I have an appointment with the President," he said. "We'll have to turn this over to some of the other members of this group. They'll explain details, Joe. Nadine's going, too. In her case, as a medical attaché in our Embassy, in Budapest. You'll go as a military observer, check on potential violations of the Universal Disarmament Pact." A sudden thought struck him. "I imagine it would add to your prestige and possibly open additional doors to you, if you carried more status." He looked again at the telly-mike on his desk. "Miss Mikhail, in my office here is Joseph Mauser, now Mid-Middle in caste. Please take the necessary steps to raise him to Low-Upper, immediately. I'll clear this with Tom, and he'll authorize it as recommended through the White House. It that clear?"

In a daze, Joe could hear the receptionist's voice. "Yes, sir. Joseph Mauser to be raised to Low-Upper caste immediately."

CHAPTER FIFTEEN

Budapest, basically, had changed little over half a millennium.

The Danube, seldom blue except when seen through the eyes of a twosome between whom spark has recently been struck, still wandered its way dividing the old, old town of Pest from the still older town of Buda. Where the stream widens there is room for the one hundred and twelve acres of Margitsziget, or Margaret Island to the West-world. Down through the ages, through Celts and Romans, Slavs and Hungs, Turks and Magyars, none have been so gross as to use Margitsziget for other than a park.

Buda, lying to the west of the Danube, is of rolling hills and bluffs and of ancient towers, fortresses, castles and walls which have suffered through a hundred wars, a score of revolutions. It dominates the younger, more dynamic, Pest which stretches out on the flat plains to the east so that though you stand on the Hármashatárhegy hill of Buda and strain your eyes, you are hard put to find the furtherest limits of Pest.

The jetport was on the outskirts of Pest, and the craft carrying Nadine Haer, Joseph Mauser and Max Mainz, settled in for a gentle landing, the autopilot more delicate far than human eye served by human hand.

Max, his eyes glued to the window, said, "Well, gee, it don't look much different than a lotta the other towns we passed over."

Nadine looked at him and laughed. She alone of the three of them had ever been outside the boundaries of the West-world having attended several international medical conventions. Over the years, the Frigid Fracas had laid its chill on tourism, so that now travel between West-world and Sov-world was all but unknown, and even visiting the Neut-world was considered a bit far out and somewhat suspect of going beyond the old time way of doing things—even among the Uppers. Securing a passport for a Middle's trip, not to speak of a Lower's, involved such endless bureaucratic red tape as to be nonsensical.

Nadine said to Joe's batman, "What did you expect, Max?"

"Well, I don't know, Miss Haer. I mean, Dr. Haer. Kind of gloomier, like. Shucks, I've seen this here town on Telly a dozen times."

"And seeing is believing," Joe muttered cynically. "It looks as though we have a reception committee." He looked at Nadine. "Are we supposed to know each other?"

She shrugged and made a moue. "It would be somewhat strange if we didn't, seeing that we flew over in the same aircraft, and were the only passengers to come this far."

He nodded and as the plane came to a halt, helped her from her chair, even as the plane's ladder slipped out and touched to the ground.

Joe grunted and said, as though to himself, "You realize that for all practical purposes there hasn't been any improvement in aircraft for a generation?"

Nadine looked at him from the side of her eyes, even as they descended. "That's what I keep telling you, Joe. We've become ossified. When a society, afraid of change, adopts a policy of maintaining the *status quo* at any cost, progress is arrested. Progress *means* change."

He grinned at her. "Sure, sure, sure. Please, no more lectures, teacher. Let what's already in my head stew a while."

On the ground, Nadine was met by one contingent from the Embassy and from the Sov-world authorities, and Joe and Max by another. Joe became occupied, hardly more than noticing that she had been whisked away in a hoverlimousine, ornately bedecked with official flags and stars.

Joe, no longer holding military rank, in spite of his mission, was in mufti, and restrained himself from returning the salute when greeted by two fresh young lieutenants from the Embassy and a be-medaled lieutenant colonel in Sov-world uniform, whose tight-waisted tunic reminded Joe of that worn by Colonel Lajos Arpád, the military attaché Joe had come across twice in West-world fracases, and who Frank Hodgson had branded an espionage agent. Joe swore again, inwardly, that these Hungarian officers must wear girdles under their uniforms, and wondered vaguely if they did so in combat.

The lieutenants, who could have been twins, so alike were they in size, bright smiling faces, uniform and words of welcome, saluted Joe, shook hands, and then turned to introduce him to the Sov-world officer.

One of them said, "Major Mauser, may we present you to Lieutenant Bela Kossuth of the Pink Army?"

They were, evidently using Joe's old title of rank, as if he were retired rather than dismissed from the Category Military. It meant little to Joe Mauser. The Sov officer clicked his heels, bowed from the waist, extended his hand to be shaken. His waist might be pinched in like that of a girl of the Nineteenth Century, but his hand was dry and firm.

"The fame of Joseph Mauser has penetrated to the Proletarian Paradise," he said, his voice conveying sincerity.

Joe shook and said, "Pink Army? I thought you called it—"

The colonel was indicating a hoverlimousine with a sweeping gesture that would have seemed overly graceful, had not Joe felt the grip of the man only a moment earlier. Kossuth interrupted him politely, "The plane was a trifle late and the banquet we have prepared awaits us, major. A multitude of my fellow officers are anxious to meet the famed Joseph Mauser. Would it surprise you to know that I have replayed, a score of times, your celebrated holding action on the Louisiana Military Reservation? Zut! Unbelievable. With but a single company of men!"

Joe was looking at him blankly. *Celebrated!* Joe couldn't but remember the fracas the mincing Hungarian was talking about. When the front had collapsed, Joe, then a captain, had held his position in the swamps while his superiors were supposedly reforming behind him, actually while they frantically tried to reach terms with the enemy.

One of the West-world lieutenants laughed at Joe's expression. "You're going to have to get used to the fact that there're as many fracas buffs over here, sir, as there are back home."

The Sov colonel waggled a finger at him. "But, no, you misunderstand completely, Lieutenant Andersen. We *study* the bloody fracases of the West. Following the campaigns of such tacticians as your Marshal Stonewall Cogswell goes far toward the training of our own Pink Army in its, ah, fracases."

That brought up a dozen questions in Joe's mind, but first he turned and indicated Max, who'd been standing behind, his eyes wide, and taking in the luxurious airport, the vehicles about it, the buildings, the airport workers, few in number though they be, the road leading to the city beyond.

Joe said, "Gentlemen, may I present Max Mainz?"

The faces of the lieutenants went blank, and one of them coughed as though apologetically.

The Sov colonel looked from Joe to Max, and then back again, his face assuming that expression so well known to Joe for so very long. The aristocrat looking at one of lower class as though wondering what made the fellow tick. Kossuth said, "But surely this, ah, chap, is a servant, one of your, what do you call them, a *Lower.*"

Max blinked unhappily and looked at Joe.

Joe Mauser said evenly, "I had heard the Sov-world was the Utopia of the proletariat. However, gentlemen, Max Mainz is my friend as well as my...assistant."

The three officers murmured some things stiffly to Max, who, a Lower born, was not overly nonplused by the situation. Zen, he knew the three were Upper caste, what was Major Mauser getting into a tissy about? He was given a seat in the front, where the chauffeur would have once been, and the others took places in the rear, one of the lieutenants dialing the hovercar's destination.

Joe Mauser said, "I am afraid my background is hazy, Colonel Kossuth. You mentioned the Pink Army. You also mentioned your own fracases. I knew you maintained an army, of course, but I thought the fracas was a West development, in fact, your military attachés are usually on the scornful side."

The two lieutenants grinned, but Kossuth said seriously, "Major, as always, nations which hold each other at arm's length, use different terminology to say much the same thing. It need not be confusing, if one digs below to find reality. Perhaps, for a moment, we four can lower barriers enough for me to explain that whilst in the West-world you hold your fracases to..." He began enumerating on his fingers. "...one, settle disputes between business competitors, or between corporations and unions. Two, to train soldiers for your defense requirements. Three, to keep bemused a potentially dangerous lower class..."

"I object to that, colonel," one of the lieutenants said hotly.

The Sov officer ignored him. "Four, to dispose of the more aggressive potential rebels, by allowing them to kill each other off in the continual combat."

"That, sir, is simply not true," the lieutenant blurted. Joe couldn't remember if he was Andersen or Dickson, even their names were similar.

Joe said, evenly, "And your alternative?"

The Hungarian shrugged. "The Proletarian Paradise maintains two armies, major. One of veterans, for defense against potential foreign foes, and named the Glorious Invincible Red Army—"

"Or, the Red Army, for short," one of the lieutenants murmured dryly.

"…And the other composed of less experienced proletarians and their techno-intellectual, and sometimes even Party, officers. This is our Pink Army."

"Wait a moment," Joe said. "What's a proletarian?"

The lieutenant who had protested the Sov officer's summation of the reasons for the West-world fracases, laughed dryly.

Kossuth stared at Joe. "You *are* poorly founded in the background of the Sov-world, major."

Joe said, "Deliberately, Colonel Kossuth. When I learned of my assignment, I deliberately avoided cramming unsifted information. I decided it would be more desirable to get my information at the source, uncontaminated by our own West-world propaganda."

One of the stiff-necked twins, both of whom Joe was beginning to find a bit *too* stereotyped West-world adherents, said, "Sir, I must protest. The West does not utilize propaganda."

"Of course not," Kossuth said, taking his turn at a dry tone. He said to Joe, "I admire your decision. Obviously, a correct one. Major, a proletarian is, well you could say, ah—"

"A Low-Lower," Andersen or Dickson said.

"Not exactly," the Sov protested. "Let us put it this way. Marx once wrote that when true Socialism had arrived, the formula would be from each according to his abilities and to each according to his needs. Unhappily, due to the fact that the Proletarian Paradise is surrounded by potential enemies, we have not as yet established this formula. Instead, it is now from each according to his abilities and to each according to his contribution. Consequently, the most useful members of our society are drawn into the ranks of the Party, and, contributing the most, are most highly rewarded. The Party consists of somewhat less than one per cent of the population."

"And is for all practical purposes, hereditary," Anderson or Dickson said.

Kossuth, in indignation, parroted, unknowingly, the lieutenant's earlier words. "That, sir, is simply not true."

Joe said, soothing over the ruffled waters, "And the…what did you call them…techno-intellectuals?"

"They are the second most useful members of society. Our technicians, scientists—although many of these are members of the Party, of course—teachers, artists, Pink and Red Army officers, and so forth."

Max looked around from the front seat. "Well, gee, that sounds just about like Uppers, Middles and Lowers to me."

Joe Mauser cleared his throat and said to the Hungarian who was glaring at Max. "And the Pink Army?"

But Kossuth bit out to Max, "Don't be silly, my man. There are no classes in the Proletarian Paradise."

"Yeah," Max said, "back in The West-world we got People's Capitalism and the people own the corporations. Yeah."

"That'll be all, Max," Joe said, getting in before the two lieutenants could snap something at the fiesty little man. Joe had already decided that the lieutenants were both Uppers, and was somewhat surprised at their lowly rank.

Kossuth brought his attention back to Joe. "We're almost to our destination, Major Mauser. However, briefly, some of the more recent additions to the Sov-world, particularly in the more backward areas of southern Asia, have not quite adjusted to the glories of the Proletarian Paradise."

Both of the lieutenants chuckled softly.

Kossuth said, "So it is found necessary to dispatch punitive expeditions against them. A current such expedition is in the Kunlun Mountains in that area once known as Sinkiang to the north, Tibet to the south. Kirghiz and Kazakhs nomads in the region persist in rejecting the Party and its program. The Pink Army is in the process of eliminating these reactionary elements."

Joe was puzzled. He said, "You mean, in all these years you haven't been able to clean up such small elements of enemies?"

Kossuth said stuffily, "My dear major, please recall that we are limited to the use of weapons pre-1900 in accord with the Universal Disarmament Pact. To be blunt, it is quite evident that foreign elements smuggle weapons into Tibet and other points where rebellion flares, so that on some occasions our Pink Army is confronted with enemies better armed than themselves. These bandits, of course, are not under the jurisdiction of the International Commission and while we are limited, they are not."

"Besides," one of the lieutenants said, "They don't want to clean them up. If they did, the Sov equivalent of the fracas buff wouldn't be able to spend his time at the Telly watching the progress of the Glorious Pink Army against the reactionary foe."

Joe, under his breath, parroted the words of the Sov officer. "That, sir, is simply not true."

Max, who had largely been staring bug-eyed out the window at the passing scene, said, "Hey, the car's stopping. Is this it?"

CHAPTER SIXTEEN

Although in actuality working on a private mission for Philip Holland, Frank Hodgson and the others high in government responsibility who were planning fundamental changes in the West-world, Joseph Mauser was ostensibly a military attaché connected with the West-world Embassy to Budapest. As such, he spent several days meeting embassy personnel, his immediate superiors and his immediate inferiors in rank. He was, as a newcomer from home, wined, dined, evaluated, found an apartment, assigned a hovercar, and in general assimilated into the community.

Not ordinarily prone to the social life, Joe was able to find interest in this due to its newness. The citizen of the West-world, when exiled by duty to a foreign land, evidently did his utmost to take his native soil with him. Even house furnishings had been brought from North America. Sov food and drink were superlative, particularly for those of Party rank, but for all practical purposes all such supplies were flown in from the West. Hungarian potables, not to mention the products of a dozen other Sov political divisions including Russia, were of the best, but the denizens of the West-world Embassy drank bourbon and Scotch, or at most the products of the vines of California. The styles of Budapest rivaled those of Paris and Rome, New York and Hollywood, but a feminine employee of the embassy wouldn't have been caught dead in local fashions. It was a home away from home, an oasis of the West in the Sov-world.

Joe, figuring that in view of the double role, unknown even to the higher ranking officers of the embassy, he could best secure protective coloring by conforming and would have slipped into embassy routine without more than ordinary notice. But that wasn't Nadine's style.

From the first, she gloried in pörkölt, the veal stew with paprika sauce, in rostëlyos, the round steak potted in a still hotter paprika sauce, in halászlé, the fish soup which is Hungary's challenge to French bouillabaisse, and threatened her lithe figure with her consumption of rétes, the Magyar strudel. All these washed down with Szamorodni or a Hungarian Riesling, the despair of a hundred generations of connoisseurs due to its inability to travel. When liqueurs were called for, barack, the highly distilled apricot brandy which was still the national tipple, was her choice, if not Tokay Aszú, the sweet nectar wine, once allowed only to be consumed by nobility so precious was it considered.

Her apartment became adorned with Hungarian, Bulgarian and Czech antiques, somewhat to the surprise even of the few Sovs with whom she and Joe associated. It had been long years since antiques were in vogue. She dressed in the latest styles from the dressing centers of Prague, Leningrad or from the local houses, ignoring the raised eyebrows of her embassy associates.

Joe, with an inner sigh, followed along in the swath she cut, Nadine being Nadine, and the woman he loved, to boot.

His being raised in caste to Upper through the easy efforts of Philip Holland, had made no observable difference in his relationship with Nadine. Of course, she was Mid-Upper, he told himself, while he was Low-Upper. Still it was far from unknown for romances to cross such comparatively little boundary. He couldn't quite figure out why she seemed to hold him at arm's length. Months had passed since she had told him, that day, she would marry him, even though he be a Middle. But now, when he tried to get her off by herself, for a moment of intimacy between them, she avoided the situation. When he brought their personal relationship into the conversation, she switched subjects. Joe, wedded for too long to his grim profession, inexperienced in the world of the lover, was out of his element.

His Upper caste rating also made little impression on the other embassy personnel, largely because it was the prevalent rank. In dealing with the Sovs, they came into contact almost exclusively with Party members and policy was that West-world officials never be put in the position to have to work with Sovs who ranked them. Only routine office workers were drawn from Middle caste, and largely they kept to themselves except during working hours.

Joe's immediate superior turned out to be a General George Armstrong, with whom Joe had once served some years earlier when the general had commanded a fracas between two labor unions fighting out a jurisdictional squabble. Although Joe hadn't particularly distinguished himself in that fray, the general remembered him well enough. Joe, recognized as the old pro he was, was taken in with open arms, somewhat to the surprise of older embassy military attachés who ranked him in caste, or seniority.

At the first, getting organized in apartment and office, getting his feeling of Budapest, its transportation system, its geographical layout, its offerings in entertainment, he came little in contact with either the Hungarians or the other officials of the Sov world, who teemed the city. In a way it was confusion upon confusion, since Budapest was the center of sovism and the languages of Indo-China, Outer Mongolia, Latvia, Bulgaria, Karelia, or Albania were as apt to be heard on street or in restaurant, as was Hungarian.

But Joe Mauser was in no hurry. His instructions were to take the long view. To take his time. To feel his way. Somewhere along the line, a door would open and he would find that for which he sought.

In a way, Max Mainz seemed to acclimate himself faster than either Nadine or Joe. The little man, completely without language other than Anglo-American, the lingua franca of the West, whilst Joe had both French and Spanish, and Nadine French and German, was still of such persistent social aggressiveness that in a week's time he knew every Hungarian of proletarian rank within a wide neighborhood of where they lived or worked. Within a month he had managed to acquire present tense, almost verbless, jargon with which he was able to conduct all necessary transactions pertaining to his household duties, and to get into surprisingly complicated arguments as well. Joe had to give up attempting to persuade him that discretion was called for in discussing the relative merits of West-world and Sov-world.

In fact, it was through Max that Joe Mauser made his breakthrough in his assignment to learn the inner workings of the Sov-world.

CHAPTER SEVENTEEN

It was a free evening for Joe, but one that Nadine had found necessary to devote to her medical duties. Max had been gushing about a cabaret in Buda, a place named the Bécsikapu where the wine flowed as wine can flow only in the Balkans and where the gypsy music was as only gypsy music can be. Max had developed a tolerance for wine after only two or three attempts at what they locally called Sot and which he didn't consider exactly beer.

Joe said, only half interested, "For proletarians, Party members, or what?"

Max said, "Well, gee, I guess it's most proletarians, but in these little places, like, you can see almost anybody. Couple of nights ago when I took off I even seen a Russkie field marshal there. And was he drenched."

Joe was at loose ends. Besides, this was a facet of Budapest life he had yet to investigate. The intimate night spots, frequented by all strata of Sov society.

He came to a quick decision. "O.K., Max. Let's give it a look. Possibly it'll turn out to be a place I can take Nadine. She's a bit weary of the overgrown glamour spots they have here. They're more ostentatious than anything you find even in Greater Washington."

Max said, in his fiesty belligerence, "Does that mean better?"

Joe grunted amusement at the little man, even as he took up his jacket. "No, it doesn't," he said, "and take the chip off your shoulder. When you were back home you were continually beefing about what a rugged go you had being a Mid-Lower in the West-world. Now that you're over here the merest suggestion that all is not peaches at home and you're ready to fight."

Max said, his ugly face twisted in a grimace, even as he helped Joe with the jacket. "Well, all these characters over here are up to their tonsils in curd about the West. They think everybody's starving over there because they're unemployed. And they think the Lowers are, like, ground down, and all. And that there's lots of race troubles, and all."

Even as they left the apartment, Joe was realizing how much closer Max had already got to the actual people, than either he or Nadine. But he was still amused. He said, "And wasn't that largely what you used to think about things over here, when you were back home? How many starving have you seen?"

Max grunted. "Well, you know, that's right. They're not as bad off as I thought. Some of those Telly shows I used to watch was kind of exaggerated, like."

Joe said absently, "If international fracases would be won by newspapers and Telly reporters, the Sovs would have lost the Frigid Fracas as far back as when they still called it the Cold War."

The Bécsikapu turned out to be largely what Max had reported and Joe expected. A rather small cellar cabaret, specializing in Hungarian wines and such nibbling delicacies as túrós csusza, the cheese gnocchis; but specializing as well or even more so in romantic atmosphere dominated by heartstring touching of gypsy violins, as musicians strolled about quietly, pausing at this table or that to lean so close to a feminine ear that the lady was all but caressed. It came to Joe that there was more of this in the Sov world than at home. The Sov proletarians evidently spent less time at their Telly sets than did the Lowers in the West-world.

They found a table, crowded though the nightspot was, and ordered a bottle of chilled Feteasca. It wasn't until the waiter had recorded the order against Joe's international credit identification, that it was realized he and Max were of the West. So many non-Hungarians, from all over the Sov-world, were about Budapest that the foreigner was an accepted large percentage of the man-in-the street.

Max said, making as usual no attempt to lower his voice. "Well, look there. There's a sample of them not being as advanced, like, as the West-world. A waiter! Imagine using waiters in a beer joint. How come they don't have auto-bars and all?"

"Sure, sure, sure," Joe said dryly. "And canned music, and a big Telly screen, instead of a live show. Maybe they prefer it this way, Max. You can possibly carry automation too far."

"Naw," Max protested, taking a full half glass of his wine down in one gulp. "Don't you see how this takes up people's time? All these waiters and musicians and all could be home, relaxing, like."

"And watching Telly and sucking on tranks," Joe said, not really interested and largely arguing for the sake of conversation.

A voice from the next table said coldly in accented Anglo-American, "You don't seem to appreciate our entertainment, gentlemen of the west."

Joe looked at the source of the words. There were three officers, only one in the distinctive pinch-waisted uniform of the Hungarians, a captain. The other two wore the Sov epaulets which proclaimed them majors, but Joe didn't place the nationality of the uniforms. There were several bottles upon the table, largely empty.

Joe said carefully. "To the contrary, we find it most enjoyable, sir."

But Max had had two full glasses of the potent Feteasca and besides was feeling pleased and effervescent over his success in getting Joe Mauser, his idol, to spend a night on the town with him. He'd wanted to impress his superior with the extent to which he had get to know Budapest. Max said now, "We got places just as good as this in the West, and bigger too. Lots bigger. This joint wouldn't hold more then fifty people."

The one who had spoken, one of the majors who wore the boots of the cavalryman, said, nastily, "Indeed? I recognize now that when I addressed you both as gentlemen, I failed to realize that in the West gentlemen are not selective of their company and allow themselves to wallow in the gutter with the dregs of their society."

The Hungarian captain said lazily, "Are you sure, Frol, that *either* of them are gentlemen? There seems to be a distinctive *odor* about the lower classes whether in the West-world or our own."

Joe came to his feet quietly.

Max said, suddenly sobered, "Hey, major, sir...easy. It ain't important."

Joe had picked up his glass of wine. With a gesture so easy as almost to be slow motion, he tossed it into the face of the foppish officer.

The Hungarian, aghast, took up his napkin and began to brush the drink from his uniform, meanwhile sputtering to an extent verging on hysteria. The major who had been seated immediately to his right, fumbled in assistance, meanwhile staring at Joe as though he were a madman.

The cavalryman, though, was of sterner stuff. In the back of his mind, Joe was thinking, even as the other seized a bottle by its long neck and broke off the base on the edge of the table, *Now this one's from the Pink Army, an old pro, and a Russkie, sure as Zen made green apples.*

The major came up, kicking a chair to one side. Joe hunched his shoulders forward, took up his napkin and with a quick double gesture, wrapped it twice around his left hand, which he extended slightly.

The major came in, the jagged edges of the bottle advanced much as a sword. His face was working in rage, and Joe, outwardly cool, decided in the back of his mind that he was glad he'd never have to serve under this one. This one gave way to rage and temper when things were pickling and there was no room for such luxuries in a fracas.

Max was yelling something from behind, something that didn't come through in the bedlam that had suddenly engulfed the Bécsikapu.

At the last moment, Joe suddenly struck out with his left leg, hooked with his foot the small table at which the three Sov officers had been sitting and twisted quickly, throwing it to the side and immediately into the way of his enraged opponent.

The other swore as his shins banged the side and was thrown slightly forward, for a moment off balance.

Joe stepped forward quickly, precisely, and his right chopped down and to the side of the other's prominent jawbone. The Russkie, if Russkie he was, went suddenly glazed of eye. His doubling forward, originally but an attempt to regain balance, continued and he fell flat on his face.

Joe spun around. "Come on, Max, let's get out of here. I doubt if we're welcome." He didn't want to give the other two time to organize themselves and decide to attack. Defeat the two, he and Max might be able to accomplish, but Joe wasn't at all sure where the waiters would stand in the fray, nor anyone else in the small cabaret, for that matter.

Max, at the peak of excitement now, yelled, "What'd you think I been saying? Come on, follow me. There's a rear door next to the rest room."

Waiters and others were converging on them. Joe Mauser didn't wait to argue, he took Max's word for it and hurried after that small worthy, going round and about the intervening tables and chairs like an old time broken field football player.

CHAPTER EIGHTEEN

Joe Mauser had assumed there would be some sort of reverberations as a result of his run-in with the Sov officers, but hadn't suspected the magnitude of them.

The next morning he had hardly arrived at the small embassy office which had been assigned him, before his desk set lit up with General Armstrong's habitually worried face. He said, without taking time for customary amenities, "Major

Mauser, could you come to my office immediately?" It wasn't a question.

In General George Armstrong's office, beside the general himself, were his aide, Lieutenant Anderson who Joe had at long last sorted out from Lieutenant Dickson, Lieutenant colonel Bela Kossuth and another Sov officer whom Joe hadn't met before.

Everybody looked very stiff and formal.

The general said to Joe, "Major Mauser, Colonel Kossuth and Captain Petöfi have approached me, as your immediate superior, to request that your diplomatic immunity be waived so that you might be called upon on a matter of honor."

Joe didn't get it. He looked from one of the two Hungarians to the other, then back at Armstrong, scowling.

Lieutenant Anderson said, unhappily. "These officers have been named to represent Captain Sándor Rákóczi, major."

Bela Kossuth clicked his heels, bowed, said formally, "Our principal realizes, Major Mauser, that diplomatic immunity prevents his issuing request for satisfaction. However..." The Hungarian cleared his throat. "...since honor *is* involved—"

At long last it got through to Joe. His own voice went coldly even. "General Armstrong, I—"

The general said quickly. "Mauser, as an official representative of the West-world, you don't have to respond to anything as dashed silly as a challenge to a duel."

The faces of the two Hungarians froze.

Joe finished his sentence. "...I would appreciate it if you and Lieutenant Anderson would act for me."

Kossuth clicked his heels again. "Gentlemen, the *code duello* provides that the challenged choose the weapons."

General Armstrong's face, usually worried, was now dark with anger. "Choice of weapons, eh? Against Sándor

Rákóczi? If you will excuse us now, gentlemen, Lieutenant Anderson and I will consult with you in one hour in the Embassy Club and discuss the affair further. I say frankly, I have never heard of a diplomat being subjected to such a situation, especially on the part of officers of the country to which he is accredited."

The Hungarians were unfazed. Kossuth looked at his wrist chronometer. "One hour in the Embassy Club, gentlemen." The two of them clicked again, bowed from the waist, and were gone.

General Armstrong glared at Joe. "Dash it, if you hadn't been so confoundedly quick on the trigger, I could have warned you, Mauser."

Joe Mauser wasn't over being flabbergasted. "You mean to tell me," he said, "that those people still conduct duels? I thought duels had gone out back in the Nineteenth Century."

"Well, you're mistaken," Armstrong bit out. "It seems to be a practice that can crop up in any decadent society. Remember Hitler reviving it among the German universities? Well, it's all the rage now among the officers of the Sov world. Limited, however, to Party members, the lowly proletariat are assumed not to have honor."

Joe shrugged, "I'm not exactly an amateur at combat, you know."

The general snorted his disgust and turned to his aide. "Lieutenant, go find Dr. Haer for me. Then wait in the outer office until it's time for us to meet those heel-clicking Hungarians."

"Yes, sir," Andersen saluted, shot another look at Joe as though in commiseration, and left hurriedly.

"What's wrong with him?" Joe said.

Armstrong pulled open a desk drawer, brought forth a bottle and glass, poured himself a strong one and knocked it back without offering any to his junior officer. He replaced the bottle and glass and turned his scowl back to Joe. "Haven't you ever heard of Sándor Rákóczi?"

"No."

"He happens to be All-Sov-world Fencing Champion and has been for six years. He also is third from the top amongst the Red Army pistol and rifle marksmen. I once saw him put on an exhibition of trick handgun shooting. Uncanny. The man has abnormal reflexes."

The door opened and Nadine was there. "Joe," she said. "Dick Andersen says you've been challenged to a frame-up duel by Sándor Rákóczi." Her eyes hurried on to Armstrong. "George, this is ridiculous. Joe has diplomatic—"

Joe wasn't getting part of this. He broke in. "What do you mean, frame-up, Nadine? We got into a hassle in a nightspot last night."

Armstrong said. "Everybody simmer down, dash it!" His eyes went to Joe. "Sándor Rákóczi doesn't get into hassles in nightspots—not unless he's been ordered to. Captain Rákóczi is what in the old days was known as a hatchetman." He snorted in deprecation. "The Party no longer conducts purges amongst its own. Everything is all buddy-buddy now. Purges are something from the past. However, those on the very top sometimes find this unfortunate. One manner that has been devised to remove such Party members who have become a thorn in the side of the powers that be, is to have them challenged by such as Sándor Rákóczi."

Joe settled into a chair, very dumbfounded. "But that's ridiculous. *Why?* Why should they want me eliminated?"

Nadine said hurriedly, "You don't have to accept."

Joe said, "If I don't, I'll be laughed out of town. Remember that big banquet the Pink Army gave me when I first arrived? The celebrated Major Joseph Mauser fling? What happens to West-world prestige when the celebrated Joe Mauser backs down from a duel?"

General Armstrong mused, "If Mauser refuses the duel, he's right, he'll be laughed out of town. If he accepts it, and is killed, he is still removed from the scene." He looked from Joe to Nadine. "Somebody evidently doesn't want Joe Mauser in Budapest."

Pieces were beginning to fit in.

Joe looked at George Armstrong. "You're one of us, aren't you? One of the Phil Holland, Frank Hodgson group." He looked at Nadine. "Why wasn't I told? Am I a junior member or something, that I can't be trusted?"

Armstrong snorted. "You should study up on revolutionary routine, Joe. The smaller the unit of organization, the better. The fewer members you know, the fewer you can betray. Here in the Sov-world, back before the Sovs came to power, the size of their cells was five members, so the most any one person could betray was four."

The tic started at the side of Joe's mouth.

Armstrong said hurriedly. "Don't misunderstand. Your fortitude isn't being questioned. Bravery no longer enters into it. There are methods today under which nobody could hold up." He seemed to come to a sudden decision. "We can't let this take place. You'll have to back down, Mauser. Somehow, there's been a leak and your real purpose in being in Budapest is known. Very well, Phil Holland and the others will simply have to send someone else to replace you."

But Joe had had enough by now. "Look," he said. "Everybody seems to think I can't take care of myself with this foppish molly and his fancy swordsmanship. I've had fifteen years of combat."

"Joe!" Nadine said, "don't be silly. The man's a professional assassin. This is his field, not yours."

Joe said flatly, "On the other hand. I have a job to do and it doesn't involve being run out of Budapest."

General Armstrong said, "Dash it, don't go drivel-happy on us, Mauser. I've just told you, the man's the best swordsman in Europe and Asia combined, and the third best shot."

"How is he with Bowie knives?" Joe said.

CHAPTER NINETEEN

To Mauser's surprise, the Sovs actually turned up two genuine Bowie knives. He had expected the duel, actually, to have to be conducted with trench knives or some other alternative. But the Sovs, ever great on museums, had located one of the weapons of the American Old West in a Prague exhibit of the American frontier, the other in Budapest itself in an extensive collection of fighting knives, down through the ages, in a military museum.

Formally correct, Lieutenant colonel Bela Kossuth appeared at Joe Mauser's apartment three days before the duel, a case in his hands. Max, in his role as batman, conducted him to Joe, doing little to keep his scowl of dislike for the Hungarian from his face. Max was getting fed up with the airs of Sov officers; caste lines were over here, if anything, more strictly drawn than at home.

Joe came to his feet on recognizing his visitor and answered the other's bow. "Colonel Kossuth," he said.

Bela Kossuth clicked heels. He held the case before him, opened it. Two heavy fighting knives lay within. Joe looked at them, then into the other's face.

Kossuth said, "Frankly, major, your somewhat unorthodox selection of weapons has been confusing. However, we have located two Bowie knives. Since it is assumed that the two gentlemen opponents are not thoroughly familiar with, ah, Bowie knives, it has been suggested that each be given his blade at this time."

Joe got it now. Sándor Rákóczi hadn't become the most celebrated duelist in the Sov-world by making such mistakes as underrating his opponents. The weapon was new to him. He wanted the opportunity to practice with it. It was all right with Joe.

Kossuth clicked his heels again. "Our selection, unfortunately, is limited to two weapons. Since you are the challenged, Captain Rákóczi insists you take first choice."

Joe shrugged and took up first one, then the other. It had been some time since he had held one of the famous frontier weapons in his hands. When still a sergeant in the Category Military, he had once become close companions with an old pro whose specialty was teaching hand-to-hand combat. Over a period of years, he and Joe had been comrades, going from one fracas to another as a team. He had taught Joe considerable, including the belief that of all blade hand weapons ever devised, the knife invented by Jim Bowie, whose frontier career ended at the Alamo, was the most efficient.

Joe ran his eyes over the blades carefully. On the back of one was stamped, *James Black, Washington, Arkansas*. Joe had found what he was looking for, however, he pretended to examine the other knife as well, ignoring the Sheffield, England stamp of manufacture.

The Bowie knife: Blade, eleven inches long by an inch and a half wide, the heel three eighths of an inch thick at the back. The point at the exact center of the width of the blade, which curved to the point convexly from the edge, and from the back concavely, both curves being as sharp as the edge itself. The crossguard was of heavy brass, rather than steel and a further backing of brass along the heel, up to the extent where the curve toward the point began. Brass, which is softer than steel, and could catch an opponent's blade, rather than allowing it to slip off and away.

Joe balanced the weapon he had selected, and shrugged. "This one will do," he said.

Kossuth clicked the case with the remaining knife shut. He could see no difference between the two. The selection of weapons had been a formality.

Max saw him to the door and returned to the living room. He said worriedly, "Major, sir, you sure you're checked out on that thing? I've been asking around, like, and they put these duels on Telly here, just like we got fracases back home. This here Captain Rákóczi's got one whopper of a reputation. He's quick as a snake. Kinda like a freak. He can move faster than most people."

"So they've been telling me," Joe mused, balancing the frontier weapon in his hand. It had a beautiful balance, this knife so big that it could be used as a hatchet or machete.

He was still contemplating the vicious looking blade when Nadine entered. He smiled up at her, put the knife aside on the table, and came to his feet.

She looked at Max, and the little man turned and left the room.

Nadine said, "Joe, a plane is leaving this afternoon. A West-world plane for London."

Joe looked at her speculatively. "I won't be on it."

"Joe, listen. A year ago you were an individual, trying to fight your way up to Upper caste. You weren't able to make it as an individual, Joe. But now you're a member of an organization, pledged to a high ideal. Joe, the organization doesn't need martyrs at this stage. It does need good, competent, highly trained members such as Joe Mauser."

He said nothing.

Nadine stepped suddenly closer to him. Her perfume, he noted, vaguely, was new, some sweet scent found here in the Sov world, undoubtedly. It had a heady quality, or was that merely the close presence of Nadine herself?

She put her arms around his neck and pulled his head down to her level. He had never realized that Nadine Haer was this much shorter then he. She pressed the softness of her lips to his.

Then she held back a foot or two, and said into his face, desperately serious, "Does this make any difference, Joe?"

He licked the edges of his lips, carefully, "It makes a great deal of difference." His voice was thick. His arms came up behind her.

"Then you'll be on the plane?"

He shook his head.

She wrenched herself suddenly free and stood back from him, infuriated. He had never seen anyone so infuriated.

He said, "Look, darling. If I had backed out of this, the way you want, you think you'd be happy. But you wouldn't. You want a man, not a coward."

"I want a *live* man! Not a dead hero."

He shook his head stubbornly. "You mentioned the organization. All right, they sent us to do a job here. They can't move in the West-world until they know where the Sov-world stands. They can't afford an attack, a sudden heating up of the Frigid Fracas, right in the middle of the confusion of a socio-economic change. They've got to know how the

Sov-world stands, what it will do. They've got to know about this so-called underground, and the religious revival stuff out there in Siberia."

"You've been discovered," she said hotly. "They can send somebody else."

He was still stubborn. "No. There's a leak. If they send somebody else, the same thing will happen. And the next man might not be as much of a potential opponent to such as Sándor Rákóczi as even I am. If I run now, the West loses prestige, and the movement sponsored by Holland and Hodgson and the rest of us, loses prestige, too. Somewhere in Budapest, is some kind of a group that is watching us. We don't know who, or where, or what they stand for, but we can't afford to lose prestige with them."

"We're not exactly going to gain it, when and if this official assassin kills you." She looked down at the wicked knife, and shuddered. "Oh, Joe, your mercenary career is over. Miraculously, you stayed alive for fifteen years through it all. From the Rank Private all the way up to Rank Major. Now at long last, you're an Upper. You're not going to throw it all away, now."

He could say nothing.

She stamped a foot in uncharacteristic fury. "You silly clod. Suppose you do win? Don't you see? They'll simply send another killer after you. They're out to get you, Joe Mauser. Don't you see you can't win against the whole Sov-world? Next time, possibly they won't be quite so formal. Possibly a few footpads in the streets. Do you think they haven't the resources to kill a single man?"

The side of his mouth twitched. "I'm sure they have. But it will give me a few days before they come up with something else. It'd be too conspicuous if I fought their top duelist one day, and then was cut down on the streets the next."

She spun, in a fury, and all but ran from the room and from his apartment.

Joe looked after her ruefully. He growled in sour humor, "Every time matters pickle for me, my gal goes into a tissy and runs off."

CHAPTER TWENTY

As Max had said, as one of their alternatives to the fracas of the West-world, the Sovs put on Telly such duels as were fought amongst their supposedly honor-conscious officer caste. Evidently, the lower caste of the Proletarian Paradise was well on the way to its own version of bread and circuses. In fact, Joe had already wondered what their version of trank was.

But though the Telly cameramen were highly evident, and for this inordinary affair had six cameras in all, placed strategically so that every phase of the fight could be recorded, they were not allowed to be so close as by any chance to interfere with the duel itself. Spaced well back from the action, they must needs depend upon zoom lenses.

Joe Mauser and Sándor Rákóczi stood stripped to the waist, both in tight, non-restricting trousers, both wearing tennis shoes. General Armstrong and Lieutenant Andersen, on one side, and Lieutenant colonel Kossuth and Captain Petöfi, on the other, stood at the sides of their principals.

Kossuth was saying formally, "It has been agreed, then, that the gentlemen participants shall be restricted to this ring measuring twenty feet across. Seconds will remain withdrawn to twenty feet beyond it. The conflict shall begin upon General Armstrong calling *commence*, and shall end upon one or the other, or both, of the gentlemen participants falling to the ground. Minor wounds shall not halt the conflict. This is understood?"

"Yes," Joe said. He had been sizing up his enemy. The man stripped well. He was almost a duplicate of Joe's build, perhaps slightly lighter, slightly taller. Like Joe, he bore a dozen scars about his upper torso. Sándor Rákóczi hadn't worked his way to the top in the dueling world without taking his share of punishment.

Rákóczi said something curtly, obviously affirmative, in Hungarian.

Lieutenant Andersen, his open face drawn worriedly, tendered Joe his Bowie knife. Captain Petöfi proffered Rákóczi his. The two men stepped into the arena, which had been floored with sand, its dimensions marked with blue chalk. Though nothing had been said, it was obvious that if a combatant stepped over this line he would have lost face.

They stood at opposite sides of the arena, both with arms loose at their sides, both holding their fighting knives in their right hands.

General Armstrong said, his voice tight and worried, "Ready, Captain Rákóczi?"

The Hungarian used his affirmative word again.

"Ready, Major Mauser?"

"Ready," Joe said. He felt like adding, *as ready as I'm ever going to be.* He was feeling qualms now. He'd been too long in the game not to recognize a superlative opponent when he saw one.

The four seconds drew back their twenty feet and joined the two doctors and half dozen hospital assistants who were there. Further back still, Joe knew, were emergency facilities. Two men by contemporary usage were going to be allowed to butcher each other, but moments after, all the facilities of modern medical science were going to be at their disposal. Joe felt a wry twinge of humor at the incongruity of it.

General Armstrong called, "Commence!"

Joe spread his legs, grasped the knife so that his thumb was along the side of the blade and held approximately waist high. He shuffled forward, slowly, feeling the consistency of the sand. There must be no slipping.

The Sov officer had assumed the stance of a swordsman. His smile was foxlike. For the first time, Joe noticed the scar along the other's cheek. It was white now, which brought it into prominence. Yes, Sándor Rákóczi, in his time, had copped one more than once. At least the man wasn't infallible.

As they came cautiously toward each other, the Hungarian grinned, fox-fashion, and said in his heavily accented Anglo-American, "Ah, our bad man from the West, you thought to choose a weapon unknown to Rákóczi, eh? But perhaps you have never heard of the Italian short sword, eh? Do you think this clumsy weapon is so different from the Italian short sword, eh?"

Joe had never heard of the Italian short sword, though now it came back to him that some of the phony-fracas films he had seen back home had depicted medieval duelists fighting with two swords, one long, one short. Obviously, his Sov opponent was thoroughly familiar with the usage. Joe swore inwardly.

They circled, warily, watching for an opening, sizing up the other. Each knew that once action was joined, events would most likely progress quickly. The Bowie knife was not built for finesse.

Like a flash, Sándor Rákóczi darted in, his blade flicked, he leapt back, instantly on guard again. There was a streak of red down Joe's arm.

Joe blinked. Somebody, General Armstrong, or was it Max? had said there was something freakish about this Hungarian. His reflexes were unbelievably fast. Now, Joe could believe it.

He attempted a slashing blow himself, and the other danced away so quickly that Joe had not come within feet of his opponent.

Rákóczi laughed insinuatingly. "Oaf," he said. "Is that the word? Clumsy, awkward, stumbling...oaf. It is well to rid the world of such, eh?"

He was a talker. Joe had met the type before, especially in hand-to-hand combat. They talked, usually insultingly, sometimes bringing up such matters as your legitimacy, or the virtue of your wife or sister, or your own supposed perversions. They talked, and by so doing hoped to enrage you, provoke you into foolish attack. Joe was untouched by such tactics. He circled again, his mind moving quickly.

He had, he realized, no advantages on his side. He was neither stronger nor faster than the other, and he had no reason to believe that he had greater stamina. If anything, it might be the other way.

Rákóczi was in again, through Joe's guard, darting his blade as though it were a foil. A cut opening magically on Joe's chest from the left nipple to navel, and bled profusely.

The Sov duelist was back a good six feet, and laughing openly. Joe had had insufficient time even to move one foot in retreat at the other's offensive.

Joe Mauser wet his lips. The tic at the side of his mouth was in full evidence.

Rákóczi jeered, "Ah, my bad man from the West who throws wine in the face of gentlemen. You grow afraid, eh? Your mouth twitches. You feel in your stomach the fear of death, eh? No longer do you worry about locating the Sov-world underground and helping to overthrow the Party, eh? Now you worry about death."

Joe tried rushing him, plowing through the sand. But the Hungarian danced back, still jeering. He obviously knew the feel of sand beneath foot, as Joe did not. Joe had no time to wonder over Armstrong and Andersen agreeing to a sand deep arena. They had messed up on that one. For Joe, it was like trying to operate on a sandy beach, but Rákóczi seemed in his element.

Even as Joe's attack slowed in frustration, the other darted in, slashed once, twice, scoring on Joe's left arm, once, twice.

He has beginning to resemble a bloody mess. None of the wounds were overly deep, but combined they were costing him blood. He got the feeling that the Hungarian could finish him off at will. That Rákóczi had his number. That it was no longer a matter of the other being careful not to underestimate the foe. Joe had been correctly estimated and found wanting. He realized that only by sinking to the sand could he throw the fight. The duel ended upon one combatant or the other falling to the sand.

And then he could see the other's expression. There was to be no throwing in of the towel for Joe Mauser. At the first sign of such a move, the other would dart in, cobra-quick, and deal the finishing blow. The death blow. Rákóczi was fully capable of such speed. The man was a phenomenon, metabolically speaking.

Joe, his heels almost to the chalk line of the arena boundary, dashing suddenly forward again. His opponent, jeering, as before, darted backward with such speed, even through the sand, as to be unbelievable.

Joe Mauser grinned wolfishly. He tossed the Bowie knife suddenly into the air. It turned in a spin to come down blade in his hand.

He stepped forward with his left foot, threw with full might. The Bowie knife, balanced to turn once completely in thirty feet, blurred through the air and buried itself in the Hungarian's abdomen, up to the hilt.

The Sov officer grunted in agony, stared down at the protruding hilt unbelievingly. His eyes come up in hate, glaring at Joe who stood there across from him, hands now extended forward in the stance of a karate fighter.

Joe could follow the other's agonized thoughts in his expression. There were medics available and though the wound was a decisive one, it need not be fatal, not in this day of surgery and antibiotics. No, not fatal, the Sov Officer decided. He glared at Joe again, his teeth grinding in his pain and shock. To move across the ring at the American would be disastrous, stirring the heavy Bowie knife in his intestines.

Rákóczi knew he had only split seconds, then he must sink to the sand so that aid might come. But perhaps split seconds were sufficient. He reversed his own knife in hand, preparatory to throwing.

Joe watched him. The other's face was a mask of pure agony, but he was no quitter. He was going to make his own throw.

It came, blurringly fast, too fast to avoid. The heavy frontier knife turned over half in the air and struck Joe along the side, glancing off, ineffectively. Sándor Rákóczi fell to the sand and the medics came on the run, both toward him and to Joe.

And then the fog began to roll in on Joe Mauser, and he noted, as though distantly, that the medical assistance that General Armstrong had provided from the West-world Embassy was headed by Dr. Nadine Haer, who seemed to be crying, which was uncalled for in a doctor with a patient, after all.

CHAPTER TWENTY-ONE

His wounds were clean, straight slashes not overly deep and which should heal readily enough. In his time, Joe Mauser had copped many a more serious one. However, after bandaging, Nadine relegated him to the small embassy hospital. The West-world diplomats would not even trust the Sov-world medical care, preferring to import their own Category Medicine personnel.

He was, so Max informed him, the lion of the West-world colony in Budapest. And the Neut-world too, for that matter. It was quite a scandal that a diplomatic representative had been challenged to a duel by a known killer of Rákóczi's reputation. Informal protests were lodged. Joe, cynically, could imagine just how effective they would be, particularly at this late date.

A lion he might be, but Nadine was not allowing him visitors this first day of his recuperation. Max, to attend him, but no others. At least, so it was throughout the morning and early afternoon. Then, so obvious was it that his hurts were not of paramount importance, she relented to the extent of allowing General Armstrong to enter.

The general scowled down at him, as though to read just how badly Joe was feeling. He grumbled, finally, "Dash it, you looked nothing so much as an overgrown hamburger steak there for a while, Mauser."

Joe grinned wryly, "It's how I felt," he said. "I've never seen anyone move so fast."

Armstrong said curiously, "If you wanted to use throwing knives, why didn't you challenge him to a duel with throwing knives?"

Joe shifted his shoulders. "I figured my only chance with him was to use a weapon with which he wasn't familiar. The Bowie knife was it. It didn't occur to him that a knife build in that shape and as big as that, was a precisely constructed throwing knife as well as one to use hand to hand." Joe twisted his mouth. "Besides, if the Sovs think all the Machiavellians are on their side, they're wrong. Poor Captain Rákóczi got sucked in. *I* had a throwing knife, but he didn't."

Armstrong looked at him blankly.

Joe explained. "The knife designed by Jim Bowie was made by a smith named James Black, of Washington, Arkansas. Bowie made himself so notorious with it that the blade became world famous and Black made quite a few exact copies. Various other outfits tried to duplicate his work, but actually none succeeded in producing the perfect balance in such a large knife that made it practical for throwing. It turns over once in thirty feet, exactly. All I had to do was to get Rákóczi fifteen feet away from me, and he'd had it. And his own knife, when he tried to reciprocate, was off balance."

Armstrong said, "Zen!"

"By the way, how is he?" Joe said.

Armstrong said, soberly, "He's dead, Mauser."

"Dead! With all those doctors standing around?"

The general's face assumed its habitually worried expression "I rather doubt he died of your knife. The highest echelons of the Party do not approve of failures. You were correct when you said you would have lost prestige had you fled Rákóczi's challenge or even insisted upon your diplomatic immunity rights. As it is, the prestige has been lost on the other side. By the way, it occurs to me that no further effort will be made to eliminate you physically. It would be too blatant."

Joe said, "One of the things I wanted to talk to you about, general. While we were in there together, Rákóczi was sounding off in an effort to crack my nerve. Called me a lot of names, that sort of thing. But he also said, I'll try to repeat this exactly, *No longer do you worry about locating the Sov-world underground and helping overthrow the Party, eh?*"

Armstrong slumped down into the bedside chair. "Dash it! That makes it definite. They're fully aware of your mission, though they haven't got it exactly right. Your purpose isn't to aid the local underground but merely to size it up, get the overall picture." He snorted his disgust. "I'll have to get in touch with our organization in Greater Washington. One thing certain, we're not going to be able to let you go into the field in your status as military attaché and observer."

Joe had been scheduled to observe some of the combat taking place in Chinese Turkestan with nomad rebels. He had looked forward to the experience, in view of his own background, wondering in what manners the Sov forces of the Pink Army differed from the mercenary armies of the West-world. He said now, "Why not?"

Armstrong snorted. "You'd never come out alive. There's be an accident, and the nomads would be given the dubious credit for having killed you." He came to his feet again. "I've got to think about this. I'll drop in later, Mauser."

Joe thought about it too, after the other had left. Obviously, the restrictions on his movements were a growing handicap on his abilities to serve the organization headed by Holland Hodgson. He wondered if he was becoming useless.

Max stuck his head in the door and said, "Major, sir, one of these here Hungarians wants to see you."

"Who?" Joe growled. "And why?"

"It's that Lieutenant Colonel Kossuth one, sir. I told him Doc Haer said you couldn't be bothered, but he don't seem to take no for an answer."

Kossuth, Joe Mauser knew, was assigned to the West-world Embassy military attaché department on a full time basis. It occurred to him that the Hungarian would be privy to the inner workings of the Party as they applied to Joseph Mauser and his associates.

"Show him in," he told Max.

"But the Doc—"

"Show him in, Max."

Lieutenant Colonel Bela Kossuth was solicitous. He clicked heels, bowed from the waist, inquired of Joe's well being.

Joe wasn't feeling up to military amenities after his framed-up near demise of the day before. He growled, "I'd think you'd be wishing I occupied Captain Rákóczi's place, rather than offering me sympathy."

The Hungarian's eyebrows went up, and uninvited he took the chair next to the bed. "But why?"

"You *were* the man's second."

Kossuth was expansive. "When asked to act, I could hardly refuse a brother officer. Besides, my superiors suggested that I take the part. As you probably have ascertained, major, there is considerable doubt the desirability of you remaining in Budapest."

Joe was astonished. "You mean to sit there and deliberately admit the duel was a planned attempt to eliminate me?"

The colonel coolly looked about the room. "Why not, major? There is no one here to witness our conversation."

"And you admit that your precious Party, the ruling organ of this Proletarian Paradise of yours, actually orders what amounts of assassination?"

Kossuth examined his finger nails with studied nonchalance. "Why not admit it? The party will do literally anything to maintain itself in its position, major. Certainly, the death of a junior officer of the West-world means nothing to them."

"But aren't you a Party member yourself?"

"Of course. One must be, if one is to operate as freely as circumstance allows in this best of all possible worlds, this paradise of ours."

Joe sank back on his pillow. He couldn't get used to the idea of this man, whom he had always thought of as the arch-stereotype Sov-world officer, speaking in this manner.

Kossuth crossed his legs comfortably. "See, here, major, you are all but naive in your understanding of our society. Let me, ah, brief you, on the history of this part of the world, and the organization which governs it. Have you studied Marx and Engels?"

"No," Joe said. "I've read a few short extracts, and a few criticisms, or criticisms of criticisms of short extracts. That sort of thing."

Kossuth nodded seriously. "That's all practically anybody does any more, even in the Sov-world where we give lip service to them. The point I was about to make is that the supposed founders of our society had nothing even remotely approaching this in mind when they did their research. It evidently never occurred to either that the first attempts to achieve the..." The Hungarian's voice went dry. "...glorious revolution, would take place in such ultra-backward countries as Russia and China. The revolution of which they wrote presupposedly a highly industrialized, technical economy. Neither Russia nor, later China had this. The, ah, excesses that occurred in both countries, in the mid-Twentieth Century, were the result of efforts to rectify this. You follow me? The Party, in power as a result of the confusion following in one case the First World War, and in the second case, the Second World War, tried to lift the nations into the industrial world by the bootstraps."

The colonel cleared his throat. "Let us say that some elements resisted the sacrifices the Party demanded—the peasants, for instance."

Joe said, dryly himself, "If I am correctly informed on Sov-world history, you do not exaggerate."

"Exactly. Let us admit it. Stalin, in particular, but others too, both before and following him, were ruthless in their determination to achieve industrialization and raise the Sov-world to the level of the most advanced countries."

Joe said, "This isn't exactly news to me, colonel."

"Of course not. Bear with me, I was but making background. To accomplish these things, the Party had to, and did, become a strong, ruthless, even merciless organization, with all power safely—from its viewpoint, of course—in its hands. And, in spite of all handicaps and setbacks, eventually succeeded in the task it had set itself. That is the achieving of an industrialized nation."

The Hungarian pursed his lips. "But then comes the rub. Have you ever heard, Major Mauser, of a ruling class, caste, clique, call it what you will, which stepped down from power freely and willingly, handing over the reins of government to some other element?"

Joe vaguely remembered hearing similar words from some other source in the not too distant past, but by now he was fully taken up by the astonishing Sov officer. He shook his head, encouraging the other to continue.

Kossuth nodded. "They tell me that in ancient Greece and Rome, tyrants or dictators would assume full powers for a period long enough to meet some emergency, and would then relinquish such power. I do not know. I would think it doubtful. But whether or not such was done in ancient Greece, it has been a rare practice indeed, since.

"A ruling caste, like a socio-economic system itself, when taken as a whole, instinctively perpetuates its life, as though a living organism. It cannot understand, will not admit, that it is ever time to die."

The Hungarian waggled a finger at Joe. "At first, when there was insufficient even of the basics such as food, clothing and shelter, Party members soon learned to take care of their own, explaining this deviation from the original Party austerity, by various means. Nepotism reared its head, as always, almost from the very beginning. Party members wished their children to become Party members and saw to it that they secured the best of education, and the best of jobs. And...how do you Americans put it...the practice of you scratch my back and I'll scratch yours, became the rule. Soon we had a self-perpetuating hierarchy, jealous of its position, and jealous of the attempts of outsiders to break into the sanctified organization. Marx and Engels wrote that following the revolution the State would wither away." The colonel laughed acidly. "Instead, in the Sov-world it continually strengthened itself. A New Class, as the Yugoslavian Milovan Djilas called it, had been born."

The Hungarian seemed to switch subjects slightly. "And a new development manifested itself. At first, Russia alone was of the Sov-world but as she became increasingly powerful, she exported her revolution, taking over in such advanced countries as, let us say, Czechoslovakia and East Germany. Here, supposedly, would have been the conditions under which the original ideas of Marx and his collaborator would have flourished, but the Party moved in its heavy bureaucracy and prevented any such development."

Bela Kossuth laughed gently. "Ah, ha, but this led to one of the ironies of fate, my friend. Because as the Sov-world expanded its borders it assimilated peoples of far more, ah, sharpness, shall we say? than our somewhat dour Russkies. In time, bit by bit, inch by inch, intrigue by intrigue—"

"I know," Joe said. "The capital of the Sov-world is now not Moscow, but Budapest."

"Correct!" the Hungarian beamed. "At the very first, we Hungarians tried to fight them. When we found we couldn't prevail, we joined them—to their eventual sorrow. However, the central problem has not been erased. We have finally achieved, here in the Sov-world, to the point where we have the abundant life. The affluent society. But we have also reached stagnation. The Party, like a living organism, refuses to die. Cannot even admit that its death is desirable."

He held his hands out, palms upward, as though at an impossible impasse.

Joe said, suddenly, "What's all this got to do with me, Colonel Kossuth?"

The Hungarian pretended surprise. "Why, nothing at all, Major Mauser. I was but making conversation. Small talk."

Joe didn't get it. "Well, why come here at all? Max said you were rather insistent about seeing me, in spite of doctor's orders."

"Ah, yes, of course." The Sov officer came to his feet again and clicked his heels. "My superiors have requested that I deliver this into your own hands, as well as copies to the West-world Ambassador, to General Armstrong and Dr. Haer." He handed a document to Joe.

Joe turned it over in hand, blankly. It was in Hungarian. He looked up at the other.

Lieutenant Colonel Bela Kossuth said formally, "The government of the Sov-world has found Major Joseph Mauser, Dr. Nadine Haer, and General George Armstrong, *persona non grata*. As soon as your health permits, Major, it is requested that you leave Budapest and all the lands of the Sov-world, never to return."

He clicked his heels, bowed again, and started for the door. Just as he reached it, he turned and said one last thing to Joe Mauser.

XXII

In spite of Nadine Haer's protests, Joseph Mauser insisted that they abide by the Sov government's expulsion order on the following day. A special plane took them to London, and they there caught the regular shuttle to Greater Washington. At least, Joe, Nadine and Max did, General Armstrong remained on in London.

The flight itself was largely uneventful, Joe having retreated into his thoughts. He had a great deal to think about. Not only in regard to the immediate collapse of his mission, but both of the past and future, as well.

Max, looking out the plane's window as they took off, bore an air of nostalgia. "Look there," he pointed. "You can see that big statue of the Magyar warriors, there in front of the Szepmuveszeti Museum, like." He sighed. "I had a date with a Croat girl, to meet her there tomorrow night. I was making good time with Carla. She thought it was romantic, me being from the West, and all."

"Max, my friend," Joe growled. "Save us the lurid details of your romances."

But his voice hadn't really borne irritation. Max went on, "You know, you kind of get used to these people. They aren't much different, like, than us. Take fracases, for instances. They don't have them like we do, but they got their Telly teams out there in Siberia, with the lads that go chasing the rebels and all. And they got their duels they cover on Telly. But I was thinking, why don't they get modern and have real fracases, like us? And then we could have, like, international meets, and they'd send a division, and we'd send one, and have it out. Zen! That'd be really something to watch."

Joe winced.

Nadine said, "Max, it took the human race ten thousand years to put even a temporary halt to the international war, now you want to bring it back for the sake of a sadistic Telly show."

"Yeah, but gee—"

Joe Mauser said, "Max, go on back to the bar and have yourself a drink. I want to talk to Nadine."

When the little man was gone, Joe said, in a conversational tone, "We can be married tomorrow, right after we've reported to Phil Holland and the others."

Her eyes widened, "Well, really! Don't you think you might ask me about it?"

He shook his head. "No, we've covered all the preliminaries. The trouble with me has been that I've continued to look *up* at you. I suppose the caste system is too deeply ingrained in me. But now...you're my woman. Period. I suppose you've actually been wondering why I've been such a slow clod."

"Do you think you're looking *down* at me now?" She countered indignantly.

"No. Just evenly. We'll be married as soon as possible."

Her voice went strangely demure. "Yes, Joe," she said.

They drove immediately from the airport to the office of Philip Holland, stopping only long enough for Joe to make a phone call.

They retraced the route over which Nadine had taken him that day that seemed so long ago, but actually wasn't. Through the long corridors, and eventually to the small office with the receptionist.

Miss Mikhail said, brightly, "Dr. Haer, Major Mauser, Mr. Holland is expecting you. Go right in."

Just before pressing through the door, Nadine put her hand on Joe's arm and looked into his face ruefully.

"Darling, you've had so much hard luck in your time, I'm sorry this first assignment for the organization had to be a failure."

Joe wet his lips, carefully, "Why'd you think it was?" he said, opening the door.

Nadine could only stare as he ushered her into Phil Holland's presence.

That crisp, efficient operator made much the same motions he had the first time Joe had met him here. Holding a chair for Nadine, shaking hands briskly with Joe and motioning to another chair for him. While they were getting settled, Frank Hodgson sauntered in, seemingly as lackadaisical and disinterested as ever. After a minimum of exchanged pleasantries, he subsided onto the couch and fished for pipe and tobacco.

Holland took in Joe's arm, still immobilized in a sling, and the other signs of his wounds. He said crisply, "I thought that we had removed you permanently from the field of combat, Joe."

Joe said sourly, "Some of the Sovs thought otherwise."

Holland said, an element of irritation in his voice, "It is hard to understand how you could have revealed yourself so quickly."

Joe pursed his lips and looked at Nadine. He said, "I think I've figured that out. It's practically impossible for Nadine to dissimulate. And I've never seen her and her brother together but that they weren't arguing."

Nadine was frowning at him. "What has Balt to do with it?"

Joe said, "I have a sneaking suspicion that in the heat of one of your arguments with your brother, the Baron, you revealed your, and my, mission and its real purpose."

Nadine's right hand went to her mouth.

Joe finished with, "And the Baron, after all, is a member of the Nathan Hale Society. I have no doubts that the organization has some connections with their equal number in the Sov-world."

Holland grunted. "Very possible. However, it's done now. The thing is, what is your opinion Joe, and yours, Nadine, on the advisability of sending other operatives on the same mission?"

Joe shook his head. "Unnecessary."

Frank Hodgson paused in lighting his pipe, to peer through the smoke.

Joe said, "In fact, it was unnecessary to send Nadine and me."

Holland's voice was testy. "I assure you, Joe, the particular assignment was quite important. We simply cannot afford to move, here in the West, until we know what the Sov-world will do. Your task was a delicate one, obviously. You simply couldn't go to their government and ask. There are strong elements in not only the Upper caste, but even the middle and Lower ones, here in this country, who would spring to the defense of present West-world society if they thought an attempt was being made to alter its structure. If the Sov government reported that it had been approached by elements of a revolutionary group, the fat would be in the fire."

Joe nodded. "I realize all that."

"You were expected to worm your way into their circles, to feel them out. To contact their own underground, if one exists. To ferret out definite information on how they would react if we began definite changes in the *status quo* here."

Joe continued to nod.

Holland was increasingly irritated. "Then why, good heavens, do you say your mission was unnecessary?"

"Because they had already sent a mission over here to contact us," Joe told him, evenly.

Had he suddenly got up from his chair, walked up the wall, across the ceiling, then down the other wall, they could not have stared at him the more.

The telly-mike on Phil Holland's desk squeaked something, and he took time enough to snap, "No. I told you, Miss Mikhail, I was not to be disturbed by *anyone*."

But Joe said, "If that's Colonel Lajos Arpád, I suggest you have him in. I took the liberty of phoning him and asking that he meet us here."

Frank Hodgson was the first to recover. "Arpád! That spy! I've just about gathered enough dope on him to have him declared *persona non grata* and ship him back to Budapest."

"As I was shipped back to Greater Washington," Joe said dryly. "Colonel Arpád and I seem to duplicate each other's activities in almost everything."

Phil Holland said crisply into the communicator, "Ask the colonel to come in, Miss Mikhail."

Ever the correct Sov-world officer, Colonel Arpád came to attention immediately upon entering the room, clicked heels, bowed from the waist. Except for Joe Mauser, none of them had met him, but he evidently knew all, greeting them by name.

The men had come to their feet. Joe said, "Meet Colonel Lajos Arpád, high in the ranks of the Sov-world Party, and at present on secret mission from the Sov-world underground revolutionary organization." Joe ended up wryly. "His mission being to determine what action the West-world might take if the secret group which has determined to make basic changes in the Sov-world socio-economic system was to take action."

It was the Hungarian who stared now. His eyes bored into Joe's face. "I do not, of course, admit that, Major Mauser. But where in the world did you receive that strange opinion?"

Joe sat down again. The blood he had lost still bothered him, and he tired easily.

He said, "From Colonel Kossuth, in Budapest. Another high ranking member of your group." Joe's eyes went back to Holland and Hodgson. Quick minded these two might be, but they were being asked to assimilate some shocking information.

Joe brought it all out. "I don't know why it didn't occur to any of us that the problems of the West-world and those of the Sov-world, at long last have become similar, almost identical. Both, following different paths, have achieved the affluent society, so called. But in doing it, both managed to inflict upon themselves a caste system that perpetuated itself, eventually to the detriment of progress. In the past, revolutions used to be accomplished by the masses, pushed beyond the point of endurance. A starving lower class, trying to change the rules of society so as to realize a better life. But now, in neither West nor in the Sov-world are there any starving. The majority of Lowers and Proletarians are well clothed, fed and housed, and bemused by fracases and trank pills, or their equivalent over there."

Joe shrugged, the weariness growing. Possibly Nadine had been right, he shouldn't have traveled so soon. "The best elements in both countries have finally realized that changes must be made. These elements, the more capable, more competent, more intelligent, already *are running* each country though they are not necessarily Uppers or Party members. Phil Holland here, supposedly a Middle secretary to the Foreign Minister, actually has performed that worthy's work for several administrations. Frank Hodgson is the working head of the Bureau of Investigation, though only a Middle. I assume a similar situation prevails in Budapest."

Arpád still stood. "It does."

Joe came to his feet, looking to Nadine. He said, "Gentlemen, I evidently have not recovered from my recent duel as much as I thought. I had better retire. Meanwhile, I suggest you exchange some notes."

Nadine hurried to his side, worried.

Holland, Hodgson and Arpád were staring at each other, somewhat like small boys, or strange dogs.

Hodgson grumbled, his voice, for once, forgetting to express laziness, "Our records show you to be a Sov espionage agent."

The Hungarian nodded, equally suspicious. "That is my official position. But I am also secretly a member of the executive committee of the organization of which Major Mauser speaks and have been attempting for some time to get in touch with the West-world underground, if one existed. I had about come to the conclusion that no such group was in existence, until today."

Joe said, "Relax boys, and let down your hair. You've got a lot in common. It looks as though, at long last, the Frigid Fracas is beginning to fade away."

THE END

If you've enjoyed this book, you will not want to miss these terrific titles...

ARMCHAIR SCI-FI & HORROR DOUBLE NOVELS, $12.95 each

D-41   **FULL CYCLE** by Clifford D. Simak
          IT WAS THE DAY OF THE ROBOT by Frank Belknap Long

D-42   **THIS CROWDED EARTH** by Robert Bloch
          REIGN OF THE TELEPUPPETS by Daniel Galouye

D-43   **THE CRISPIN AFFAIR** by Jack Sharkey
          THE RED HELL OF JUPITER by Paul Ernst

D-44   **PLANET OF DREAD** by Dwight V. Swain
          WE THE MACHINE by Gerald Vance

D-45   **THE STAR HUNTER** by Edmond Hamilton
          THE ALIEN by Raymond F. Jones

D-46   **WORLD OF IF** by Rog Phillips
          SLAVE RAIDERS FROM MERCURY by Don Wilcox

D-47   **THE ULTIMATE PERIL** by Robert Abernathy
          PLANET OF SHAME by Bruce Elliot

D-48   **THE FLYING EYES** by J. Hunter Holly
          SOME FABULOUS YONDER by Phillip Jose Farmer

D-49   **THE COSMIC BUNGLERS** by Geoff St. Reynard
          THE BUTTONED SKY by Geoff St. Reynard

D-50   **TYRANTS OF TIME** by Milton Lesser
          PARIAH PLANET by Murray Leinster

ARMCHAIR SCIENCE FICTION CLASSICS, $12.95 each

C-13   **SUNKEN WORLD**
          by Stanton A. Coblentz

C-14   **THE LAST VIAL**
          by Sam McClatchie, M. D.

C-15   **WE WHO SURVIVED (THE FIFTH ICE AGE)**
          by Sterling Noel

ARMCHAIR MASTERS OF SCIENCE FICTION SERIES, $16.95 each

MS-5   **MASTERS OF SCIENCE FICTION, Vol. Five**
          Winston K. Marks—Test Colony and other tales

MS-6   **MASTERS OF SCIENCE FICTION, Vol. Six**
          Fritz Leiber—Deadly Moon and other tales

If you've enjoyed this book, you will not want to miss these terrific titles…

ARMCHAIR SCI-FI & HORROR DOUBLE NOVELS, $12.95 each

D-51   **A GOD NAMED SMITH** by Henry Slesar
           WORLDS OF THE IMPERIUM by Keith Laumer

D-52   **CRAIG'S BOOK** by Don Wilcox
           EDGE OF THE KNIFE by H. Beam Piper

D-53   **THE SHINING CITY** by Rena M. Vale
           THE RED PLANET by Russ Winterbotham

D-54   **THE MAN WHO LIVED TWICE** by Rog Phillips
           VALLEY OF THE CROEN by Lee Tarbell

D-55   **OPERATION DISASTER** by Milton Lesser
           LAND OF THE DAMNED by Berkeley Livingston

D-56   **CAPTIVE OF THE CENTAURIANESS** by Poul Anderson
           A PRINCESS OF MARS by Edgar Rice Burroughs

D-57   **THE NON-STATISTICAL MAN** by Raymond F. Jones
           MISSION FROM MARS by Rick Conroy

D-58   **INTRUDERS FROM THE STARS** by Ross Rocklynne
           FLIGHT OF THE STARLING by Chester S. Geier

D-59   **COSMIC SABOTEUR** by Frank M. Robinson
           LOOK TO THE STARS by Willard Hawkins

D-60   **THE MOON IS HELL!** by John W. Campbell, Jr.
           THE GREEN WORLD by Hal Clement

ARMCHAIR SCIENCE FICTION CLASSICS, $12.95 each

C-16   **THE SHAVER MYSTERY, Book Three**
           by Richard S. Shaver

C-17   **THE PLANET STRAPPERS**
           by Raymond Z. Gallun

C-18   **THE FOURTH "R"**
           by George O. Smith

ARMCHAIR SCI-FI & HORROR GEMS SERIES, $12.95 each

G-5   **SCIENCE FICTION GEMS, Vol. Three**
           C. M. Kornbluth and others

G-6   **HORROR GEMS, Vol. Three**
           August Derleth and others